To my Ted, my college sweetheart, my wonderful husband and my best friend. We will always be "Siamese twins connected at the heart." I love you forever.

Accolades for author Beth Albright

The Sassy Belles—
 Top Five Summer Pick – Deep South Magazine
 Finalist: Best Debut Novel – Book Junkie Choice Awards

Wedding Belles—
 RT Magazine Top Pick for August
 Nominated for GOLD SEAL OF EXCELLENCE, RT Magazine/August

Sleigh Belles—
 Barnes and Noble Bookseller Picks: September Top Pick for Romance

PRAISE For The Sassy Belles Trilogy

Dripping with southern charm and colloquialisms, the novel once again proves Albright's firsthand knowledge of southern culture. *The women in Albright's novels are especially well written*—happy to challenge the status quo when necessary but also aware of that old adage, "You catch more flies with honey." This delightfully campy and romantic read will satisfy fans of Mary Kay Andrews, Alexandra Potter, and Lisa Jewell. **Booklist Review for** *Wedding Belles*

By turns tender, witty, steamy, and sharp, Albright's debut novel proves she's a gifted storyteller with intimate knowledge of southern culture. This charming tale is tailor-made for fans of Mary Kay Andrews and Anne George." – **Booklist Review for** *The Sassy Belles*

...with distinct nods to the strength of family, the friendship sisterhood and the indomitable Southern spirit...Albright's first novel is a frothy, frolicking story..." –**Kirkus Review for** *The Sassy Belles*

"Albright good-naturedly displays her inner redneck while steering this giddy Dixie romp with ease-leaving lots of room at the happy ending for another adventure starring these steel magnolias" –**Publisher's Weekly Review for** *The Sassy Belles*

"The Sassy Belles are back and sassier than ever! ... With clever dialogue and richly drawn characters, Albright shows once again she's a natural-born storyteller who knows how to pen a charming tale. Regardless of

game-day colors worn, this sexy and fun Southern series will have readers coming back for more!" –**RT Magazine Review for *Wedding Belles***

*"**The Sassy Belles** reminded me that the South is like no other place on earth. Kudos to Beth Albright for capturing its spirit so perfectly in this lighthearted debut novel."* -Celia Rivenbark, New York Times bestselling author of *We're Just Like You, Only Prettier*

CHAPTER 1

The phone was ringing incessantly. Urgent. I had that sinking feeling in the pit of my stomach as I spread my legs and heaved myself up from the front porch swing. I was eight months pregnant and winter had fallen on Tuscaloosa like a silent frozen night. The air outside was so cold I could see my breath. The holidays had ended and with it all the exhausting festivities. Well, everything's exhausting when you're this pregnant. We were well into February and Sonny and I had settled in for the cold, drizzly, cozy months ahead, our baby on the way. It was a bliss I had waited for as long as I could remember.

But that phone wouldn't stop. My cell was charging in the front room. I had taken a week off work at the law practice to get the house and our new nursery ready. A cup of hot chocolate was warming in my icey-cold hands. I went out to the porch to get a breath of the frigid winter air. Bruised and bloated clouds hung low, rolling over the tops of the pine trees that filled the yard. A winter storm was brewing.

I had decided to sit on the swing for a minute when my cell phone rang for the first time. I ignored it till it stopped. But then almost immediately, it rang again. I pushed the soft heavy cotton quilt off my lap while gripping my hot chocolate with my other hand. Sonny's grandmother had made the crimson and pine colored heavy blanket when he was just a boy. He was so family-oriented. The house itself had belonged to his parents. His sense of family was one of my favorite things about him. Nothing was more important to him than our little growing family.

"I'm coming I'm coming, " I yelled to the irritating ringing device. It was on its third set of rings by the time I waddled over to the leather chair near the stone fireplace and reached for the phone on the table. I didn't even look at the caller I.D. It seemed like such an emergency. I hit the answer button as I brought it up to my ear.

"Hello," I managed, a tad out of breath.

"Blake, I need to see you."

"Who is this?" I knew who it was but couldn't believe my ears.

"It's Harry, you know, your other husband."

"Harry! My God, you sound awful, and the divorce is all but final and no, I'm not married to Sonny just yet," I said sarcastically. "So there is no *other* husband."

"Blake I need to see you. I'm coming home for a week and we need to talk."

"No, Harry, we have absolutely nothing to say. Your life is in D.C. now and with whoever is your flavor of the week next to you in bed. So, nice of you to call but I'm a little busy getting on with my life." I was exasperated.

Harry and I had been married for ten years when it all fell apart last year. I was going to talk to Harry about a separation the day it all happened. But my best friend Vivi got into a bit of trouble that day and that talk never happened—at least the way I had planned. I'm an attorney, mostly taxes and estates, but my BFF Vivi was in trouble—again, and Harry and I were her attorneys. Harry and I had a law practice together. That was about all we had been doing together for an eternity. Later, in November, Harry had run for the Senate and won. He moved to D.C. right after the election.

Right or wrong I saw Sonny, my on-again-off-again high school sweetheart last summer in the middle of Vivi's investigation and the sparks were still there. But, they were more explosive now since we weren't in high school anymore. I had never felt such a sizzle as I did with him.

Sonny is rugged, a former boy scout who still prefers the lush forest or a blue, shimmering lake to an office. Even though I'm more of an indoor-girl, who loves her Jimmy Choos, the chemistry between us is crazy. I have never been so in love with anyone. Sonny and I began to see each other as my marriage dissolved under the pressures of Harry's political campaign. But truthfully, the marriage had been falling apart, little by little, for years.

For example, Harry was caught in not one but two compromising positions last summer. I had the great fortune of catching him myself. It broke my heart, but deep down I knew he was so caught up in running for office that I had become his collateral damage. Nothing was ever more important to Harry than getting that Senate seat and moving to Washington. However, seeing him with other women really ended it all. It hurt me so deeply. I mean, it was one thing to know we had grown apart but to *see* him cavorting in our home was too much. I so wish it was possible to "unsee" things!

"Please, Blake, I have to see you before it's too late," Harry pleaded.

"Too late? You're not dyin' are ya?" Silence followed.

"Harry? You still there?"

"No, Blake, I'm okay. But I think we need to have a heart to heart so to speak." He laughed a little. That was our last name, Heart. Well, it was fixin' to be my "former" last name. Sonny and I had plans to get married soon as the baby was here. He had proposed to me on New Year's Eve. The baby was due in March, next month. We already knew we had a boy on the way. A son. It warmed me at the thought. Now Harry had no place back in my life—especially right now. I was trying to nest and the baby would be here before we knew it. Plus, Harry and I were supposed to sign our final divorce papers next week. This was really bad timing hearing from him right now.

"Why, Harry? Somethin' wrong? Your constant stream of lady-friends dry up?" I asked sarcastically.

"Blake—I uhm—I well…"

"Yes, Harry? Just spit it out for God's sake."

"Blake…" I could hear him inhale a deep breath then finally, "Blake, I'm still in love with you."

CHAPTER 2

I dropped the phone as I plopped onto the over-sized dark leather couch. I had been pacing since I picked up the phone—no sense sitting since it nearly took a crane to get me up these days. The phone was on the floor and I could still hear Harry talking from somewhere between my legs. Don't think that, now. He never talked much from that angle anyway.

"Blake!" He sounded frantic, like he thought I had hung up. "Blake!" He shouted.

"Harry! I dropped the phone!" I screamed into the air, hoping he would hear me. I wriggled and squirmed, feeling for the cell phone on the wood floor between my feet until I felt it. I could also feel my face turning nearly blue as I struggled with my legs spread, bending over my huge belly searching for the cell phone. I couldn't quite position myself to grab it right away.

I kept shouting into the phone, "Harry I'm tryin' to pick it up—just a minute." Finally, I managed to pick it up, breathless and uncomfortable on so many levels.

"Harry, you are not in love with me so get over yourself. You're just being needy. Go find some floozy and you'll be back in shape in no time. Now, I'm busy getting' ready for the baby. The decorators for the nursery are coming and I got work to do. I gotta get back to my real job next week at what used to be *our* law practice and the baby's due next month. We both have moved on and everything's been said."

"No Blake, I've already booked my flight. I'll be in Tuscaloosa tomorrow. We have to talk." He hung up before I could even utter another sound.

I sat there a minute, trying to process what has just transpired. I knew he was not to be trusted but something stirred in me.

There had been a time when Harry and I had been invincible. No, I wasn't moved emotionally by this call. I was so in love with my sexy cop now I couldn't see straight. But a little bubble of melancholy swirled through me as I sat on Sonny's leather couch clutching my phone. Harry had been such an ass. A fool. He was driven beyond anyone I had ever known and at the sacrifice of anything and everything dear to him. Nothing would stand in his way to get that Senate seat. Along the way he had sacrificed us— me. I was momentarily sad for him. But only momentarily.

There was only one thing to do in times like this—call Vivi.

* * *

"He said what?" she yelled into the phone. "That stupid son-of-a-bitch better not bring his sorry ass down here unless he wants that sorry ass kicked personally by me all the way back to Washington. He was a jerk to you and to my Lewis, his very own brother, and I have yet to forgive him."

Vivi was never one to hide her feelings.

"I totally agree," I assured her. "But the thing is--he said he still loves me." I just threw it out there. I figured she couldn't yell much louder or she'd wake her baby, Tallulah. I was wrong.

"What the hell did you just say? He loves you, my big white freckled ass! Harry never loved anybody but Harry-- and whoever could get Harry elected. He's up to something Blake, but no matter what, don't you let him back into your life. You're a fool if you do."

"Oh, my God, no! I would never let go of Sonny. He's the best thing that ever happened to me. But Harry must need something back here. I mean he'll be here tomorrow."

"What are you gonna do? Meet him somewhere? I mean you have to tell Sonny, right? You *are* gonna tell Sonny. Right?"

"Of course I am. I just don't wanna upset the apple cart, ya know?"

"No, I don't know. What are you talking about?"

I heaved a deep breath. "I just thought if I could hear what Harry has to say-- make him understand there is nothing here-- then he can just go and no one has to know."

"Well, that is the very worst plan I have ever heard," Vivi huffed.

I loved Vivi. I could count on her. She was that friend who would say, "That most assuredly *does* make you look fat! Now, take it off." So I knew I needed to listen to her. I was in a pregnancy fog anyway, and now I just wanted this over. I was in the nesting mode and Harry was making a mess of it. I wanted to hide from it all together. That's it! I could leave town tomorrow and just conveniently not be here when Harry shows up.

"Okay, why?" I asked Vivi. "Why is this the very worst plan ever? I mean I think Harry's just seeing the end now.

We're supposed to sign the papers next week. Maybe he's just wanting to make sure."

"What the hell drugs are you takin"? Vivi was heading for a hissy fit and it was directed squarely at me. " Listen to me, Blake. You gotta see him and you gotta tell Sonny he's coming. You and I both know that sleazy soon-to-be-ex of yours is up to something."

"Okay, I know you're right. I'm just tired, I think. With the baby coming and all preparations I'm just in a haze. I'll…" She interrupted me.

"Oh my God! Lewis honey, what's wrong?" She was talking to her husband Lewis, Harry's brother, who was supposed to be at his radio station. He owned the station that broadcasts the Alabama football games and he was their announcer. Obviously, he had just walked in the house unexpected.

"Blake, just a minute. Lewis looks like he just got some bad news. Hang on for a second and let me see what it is." She dropped the receiver and I heard it hit something. I could hear her as she tried to talk to Lewis. "He did what?" I heard. "Oh my Lord. What in hell—okay now I get it." I heard the swishing noises as Vivi made her way back to the phone.

"Okay, now I get it." Vivi was loud and upset.

"What? What do we get?" I begged full of curiosity.

"Lewis heard from the news room at the radio station. Seems like our Harry is embroiled in a little senatorial affair—with an intern!"

CHAPTER 3

I sat wringing my hands, squirming in the seat, tapping the tabletop. I was at the T-Town café just off Fifteenth Street. The interior was so warm and inviting. The smell of their delicious fried green tomatoes had me salivating, despite my nerves. I had called Sonny to meet me for lunch.

Sonny was working on a case so I knew he didn't have much time. Someone had found an elderly man slumped over in his car on that dirt road that led out to the trailer park, the one near the river where Miss Myra Jean, the psychic lived. Sonny was on the case to determine if foul play was involved. A tough case put him in his element. I hoped my news wouldn't throw a wrench into his day. He loved his work so much and I loved watching him work. He was the Chief of Homicide for the Tuscaloosa Police Department. He looked a lot like Blake Shelton, that handsome very tall country music singer, all cuteness, muscles and dimples.

"Hey beautiful," Sonny said as he took his seat beside me near the back of the restaurant.

I loved when he said that. That was his way. He always said hello to me like this and I felt like the most beautiful woman in the world when I was with him. Sonny had a way about him --his grin, and his one eyebrow that arched when he wanted me, which was every time he looked at me. And his swagger. Oh, that swagger. Watching him walk should be a spectator sport.

I had met Sonny in the ninth grade. We were on again off again until we were twenty years old and in college. He wanted marriage, but I was hyper-focused on my law career. When we broke up the last time, as I headed to New York for an internship, the sadness and disappointment in his sweet brown eyes etched an image in my heart I never forgot. He was the boy I left at home as I stretched myself ever further into my dream-life where I met and married Harry Heart who also become my law partner.

But in the end, old feelings never really die and my heart thumped a little faster that day last year when I ran into him on a case. By then Harry and I were all but over and it felt good to see my cop. Just like it did now in the restaurant.

"Hey Baby, you're a sight for sore eyes," I breathed into his neck as he leaned down to kiss me. I inhaled his skin and his Stetson cologne, the cold air outside still clinging to his red cheeks. "What's up? You look worried or like you might throw up," he said.

"Well you know, I should be over all the morning sickness by now," I hinted.

"So I know that look, Baby. What's wrong inside that gorgeous head of yours?"

The waitress showed up with our waters and we ordered our drinks--regular Coke for me, Dr. Pepper for Sonny, his usual. I hesitated and squirmed, darting my eyes anywhere but into his.

"Come on Sugar, you can tell me anything. The baby's okay isn't he? I mean it's not the baby is it?"

"Oh no, Baby, he's just as healthy as a quarterback," I offered a reassuring smile. I knew I was making him worried so I just spilled it.

"Harry's coming here. Tomorrow."

"What for?" He asked swigging his water and crinkling his brows at me.

"He says we need to talk, but Lewis found out something today. As soon as it hits the six o'clock news tonight, the whole town's gonna know. Tuscaloosa's gonna be the very worst place Harry can be. I need to stop him, but I wanted you to know first."

"What is it? What did he do?" Sonny leaned toward me.

The restaurant had ceiling fans that churned slowly on this frigid day, just enough to swirl the mouth watering aroma of the fried chicken and red velvet cakes baking. I could live here. It all smelled so delicious. The cafeteria styled oak tables were scattered around here and there. The inviting patio full of picnic tables was closed up for the winter. The café sat right this side of the train tracks and every so often a horn could be heard. The noise was deafening. But no one seemed to care about that or even notice it, for that matter. We were all here for the delectable offerings of some of the best southern food I had ever eaten.

We ordered, and before I knew it, the waitress delivered our plates. As bad as I wanted to dig in to those famous fried green tomatoes, I knew Sonny needed the whole truth. I had hem-hawed long enough.

"Harry has been accused of having an affair."

"Huh," he let out with sarcasm and a smirk, "well, that's sure nothin' new."

"No, Baby, he's been accused of sleeping with his intern."

"Oh my God, that stupid bastard." He shook his head in both disbelief and disgust as he cut into his chicken fried steak. Then suddenly, he looked up at me. "Why the hell is he comin' here?"

I knew I had to tell him about the phone call this morning. "Harry called me this morning."

Sonny, still chewing, put his fork down and wiped his mouth with a white paper napkin. "What? Why?" he looked confused.

"He said he still loves me and we need to talk; but obviously he is running home to hide. He just wants to use me for show."

Sonny cut me off. "Kinda like he did to get elected?" Sonny was suddenly stern. "You know I'm not vindictive but I really don't want Harry bringing you down into his sleazy problems. I mean he's made his bed. It's not your fault he's had everyone and their sisters *in* that bed—or in this case their daughters. So please, don't even talk to him. It's not worth it. Want me to call him?"

That was just like Sonny—jump in and be protective.

"No, no I can handle him," I said with reassurance. I wasn't so sure myself but I had to make Sonny believe me or this whole thing could blow up before I could stop it.

We finished our lunch and Sonny got up, all six foot three of him, long legs stretched out, he slapped at his fit thighs brushing the last of the crumbs to the floor.

"I love you, Baby. Now don't stress. You and my future little quarterback surely don't need any of what Harry has to offer. I'll see you tonight and we'll get the finishing touches on that crib, okay?" He kissed me goodbye. I smiled back at him, rubbing my baby belly. Sonny was sure right about one thing; Harry had nothing to offer but trouble. But, he was already on his way, headed straight for me.

CHAPTER 4

I got home that afternoon after lunch and saw the unmistakable Pepto Bismal pink van pulled up in front of my house. The Fru Frus. They were caterers who were now trying their hands at becoming decorators—and I was their very first decorating client. The name of their little company is A Fru Fru Affair. Oh, they still did their catering. They were amazing with food. They had catered Vivi's wedding last fall and it was fabulous. Now they wanted to branch out into the world of interior design too. Sometimes I wondered if I had totally lost my mind.

Crazy did run in my family after all. Meridee, my grandmother, always said to me, *Blake, your mother is crazy.* And yes, sometimes my mother Kitty was certifiable. But there's crazy—and there's bat-shit crazy. Kitty was the good crazy.

Kitty loved to love me-- out loud. If anybody did anything wrong to me, Kitty was the queen mother of the mama-bears. I suddenly wondered what in the world she was gonna do when she saw the news about Harry! I knew I had to tell her, but first I had to deal with the decorators. The baby could be early and it scared me to death that we might not be organized and ready.

I made my way in to the house only to be greeted by the Fru Fru's. There were just the two of them. They had been together since high school when they changed their names from Craig and Jean Paul to Coco and Jean Pierre. They had opened up their own catering company right after high school while both were in culinary school. They were great chefs; the interior decorating thing was yet to be seen.

Jeanne Pierre was always dressed in dark clothes. He had dark hair and green eyes and was never without his notes and his iPad. Coco was lighter, with sandy blonde long hair and blue eyes. He was funny and even on this cold winter day he was dressed in bright blue skinny jeans and a lemon yellow striped sweater.

"Hey y'all, I'm home," I announced as I entered the house. I had given them the key so they could work on the new nursery. They had been at it for over two weeks and I wasn't allowed to even peek at it. They wanted it to be a surprise. I was hopeful as I made my way inside. Sonny and I had decided to turn an unused guest room into the baby's room.

I was so tired after my busy emotional morning all I wanted to do was have a seat with some hot cider and put my feet up. But other things were on the agenda.

"Hey baby girl!" Coco bounded in from the bedroom and kissed me on the cheek—well mostly in the air.

"Hey honey," I said. "How's it going?" I threw my red leather Kate Spade bag and keys onto the front room chair. I began to slip off my long wool red coat as Coco continued.

"Oh, girl—you are gonna so love this! We worked so hard to get it ready for you to see. You are gonna be so surprised!" He raised his eyebrows as he grasped my hand

and dragged me up the hall and back to the new nursery. "Now remember, we're still in the early stages, but we think we're on the right track. Cover your eyes and I'll count to three." Coco was so excited. I however, suddenly felt butterflies take flight in my stomach. I had given them some creative freedom. Suddenly I was seriously second-guessing my generosity.

"Now don't open your eyes till we say three, okay? Jean Pierre has his camera ready to take a picture of your reaction." Coco led me by the hand as we walked. I felt our arrival as we made a stop. He turned me to the left, so I would be right in the doorway.

" Okay, here we go," Coco said.

"One. Two. Three!" Both of them shouted in unison.

I quickly uncovered my eyes and stood speechless as Jean Pierre snapped pictures like I was on the red carpet. What I saw nearly threw me into labor! I felt my eyes bug out and my mouth drop open.

"Oh, my," I uttered. "Uhm, I do love it but somehow I think we may have mixed up the plan a tad." I was trying so hard not to hurt their feelings. But the vision I saw while standing there in the doorway made me instantly nauseous.

"Oh, honey, I thought you would love it! We went to so much trouble to make sure we got the nudes of you and Sonny just right. We were guessing, of course. I mean we couldn't ask y'all to strip down and model since it was a surprise and all," Coco said proudly.

"But I never asked for a mural of me and Sonny nude and riding bareback on a-- unicorn—over a rainbow! I mean it *is* a nursery after all and having a painting of mama and daddy naked on the wall really isn't –well, too appropriate. I'm gonna have to ask y'all to just paint the walls a buttery yellow and add those baby blue stripes. That's his colors for now--cheerful."

"Well if y'all ridin' on a beautiful unicorn over a rainbow isn't cheerful, I have no idea what is!" Jean Pierre wasn't just hurt-- he was insulted.

The Fru Fru's looked so disappointed. But, honey—me and Sonny naked--waving out from the wall, ridin' bare-butt on a glittery unicorn? Please! I could barely stomach looking at it. We looked like Siegfried and Roy, not Blake Shelton and Katy Perry. That's who I think Sonny and I look like, anyway. What am I even talking about? Me and Sonny naked on a mural had no place in a nursery, no matter what!

"Oh, it's cheerful, but not for the baby. Would y'all mind just doing the stripes for now? Maybe we can do a mural another time?" I was trying to be diplomatic.

"Bo-ring," Coco sang in a high-pitched voice. "Fine if average is what you want we are happy to please."

"Soooo not creative," Jean Pierre chimed in "but sure."

"Thanks y'all. Sweet and cheerful with an overtone of warmth. That's the idea, okay?" I reiterated.

"Sure, we get it. I'm just so disappointed you didn't like it," Coco muttered. "But, we'll do it your way. Painting over this masterpiece is gonna be such a tragedy but of course, your wish is our command," he smirked, pushing the guilt. "I'll take some pictures so we can re-create it, maybe in the family room."

Oh, Lord—how do I tell them it's plain awful?

"Uhm, no," I began," let's just hold off on the murals for now. Sonny likes all the exposed wood that is natural to the house."

Conflict avoided-- for now. Whew.

"Here, take a look at your reaction, sweetie. I just knew right away that you loved it!" Coco grabbed the iPad and showed me my face as I looked at the mural for the very first time. Yes it sure looked like I loved it—if you like a face that looks just like I had stepped in a fresh steaming pile of dog shit. 'Cause that's exactly what I looked like.

"Okay, we'll get to it tomorrow. For now just keep the door closed since it obviously isn't your taste," Coco said as he and Jean Pierre gathered their things. Just then someone walked in the house. I could hear the front door slam.

"Blake, Honey, you here?" Oh good God, it was Sonny. "I'm with Jay Johnson, you decent?"

"Oh, good! Maybe we need a second opinion," Coco suggested.

"No, no! I think it would be much better if he didn't see it." I knew Sonny would certainly have an opinion but not one they necessarily wanted to hear. And Jay—oh my God, he was head of Vice and Sonny's best friend at work. If he saw this, Sonny would never live it down. It would most assuredly get all over the station.

"Where is everybody?" Sonny sounded a little irritated.

I could hear their footsteps continue up the hallway. I reached in to try to grab the knob and pull it shut. "Hurry! Hurry!" I scurried to make everything look just right. But of course, Sonny beat me to the doorway.

"Good God Almighty!" Sonny shouted.

"Holy shit!" Jay burst into hysterics. He took out his phone and began snapping. "This is hilarious! Wait'll the guys at work get a load of this!" He kept laughing till tears rolled down his cheeks.

"See. I knew he would love it," Coco smiled giddily referring to Sonny's reaction. Clearly he misunderstood the religious references.

"What the hell is Siegfried and Roy doin' on the back of that flyin' horse—in my new baby boy's nursery? I know we didn't agree on a Vegas theme!"

"No, that's you, Sonny. Can't you tell?" Jean Pierre asked.

Sonny squinted his eyes, "I can't say that I can."

"Oh, I can. It looks just like you," Jay teased. "Especially all that chest hair. I never knew you were so sexy."

"Fine, both of y'all just have no sense of taste," Coco huffed. "We'll fix it tomorrow. Keep the door closed since it's such a eye-sore."

"Oh, that won't be a problem," Sonny chided, closing the door to stop Jay from taking any more pictures with his phone.

"Ugh! You two!" Coco shook his head. "We'll see y'all in the morning with the boring butter yellow and baby blue paint." Coco leaned over and air kissed each of my flushed cheeks. Jean Pierre went down the front stairs and started the pink van. They drove away, spitting dirt behind them. I wasn't so sure their interior-decorating career had much of a future. I could only hope my new baby would have a nursery and not a glittery Vegas show room when they got finished.

"Can we say blackmail?" Jay was still chuckling while flipping through the pictures in his phone. He held it up over his head and laughed a bit harder. "These are sure gonna come in handy next Christmas party!"

"You better delete every last one of those," Sonny threatened. He was grinning but I knew he meant it.

"What are y'all doing here?" I asked.

"I needed to pick up a report I left here and Jay and I were heading out to check in with the coroner on that old man I found," Sonny said.

"Yeah, we're kinda workin' on this one together." Jay explained. "We have a few leads so we thought we'd run over it all together."

"Okay, I'll have dinner waiting. Hurry back."

Sonny bent down and kissed my lips.

"See you in a few," I smiled sweetly. I wanted him to hurry up and leave.

I had a lot of thinking to do. Harry was on his way and Sonny didn't want me involved.

I walked them to the porch closing the front door behind them. I let out a huge deep breath as they got into Sonny's squad car.

I could hear the muffled sounds of Jay continuing to call Sonny a Vegas Act and how he had no idea how much he loved riding animals bare butt naked. I just hoped they could stay busy. I had a lot on my plate at the moment with Harry and I needed them to stay outta of my hair till I could get him back to Washington. Exactly how I was gonna to do that hadn't quite come to me yet—but it would.

CHAPTER 5

The chill in the air along with the early morning light nudged me awake. The bedroom was awash in amber earthy warmth. My nose was cold, but it was so warm under the down crimson comforter and heavy thick blankets. I snuggled under them a little deeper not wanting to face this day. Harry would be in town soon and all that thinking last night didn't get me anywhere but more and more anxious.

Sonny had left early headed out to the trailer park to see if he could find any more clues on that old man. So, I turned over and pulled the toasty covers up around my face hoping to catch a bit more sleep when someone banged on the front door. I turned over again not wanting to believe anybody would actually be up, dressed, and out for a visit this early.

"Blake! Sweetheart, it's your mother! Get up and let me in! I'm freezing my big ass off out here." It was Kitty, my mother the real estate agent who was fixin' to marry our dear mayor, her fifth try at matrimony. But who's still even counting? Oh, lord have mercy. What did she want at this ungodly hour? Maybe it was a nightmare. I snuggled down a little more but the loud wrapping came again. Oh no, I thought to myself. I had forgotten to tell her about Harry. Here it comes.

"Okay, okay, Mother! I'm coming!" I threw on my thick, warm, baby blue robe and slid into my fuzzy slippers and made my way to the front door, flinging it open. In marched Kitty, her arms flying, her bangles jingling.

"Lord have mercy, Blake, have you seen the newspaper?" I didn't have to answer as she was waving it over her head as she flew in from the porch. "What the hell is he doing? Wrecking our plans to keep him in Washington forever? Good God, that man needs to keep it in his pants. When is he ever gonna learn?"

"Mother, he's on his way here." I knew that would go over well.

"He's what? Well, he's not welcome here. Baby girl, you've got to distance yourself from him or he's gonna drag you right down under the ship when it sinks."

"Thank you, Mother for the fantastic advice. He called me yesterday and told me he still loves me." Canon ball number two. I knew I was toying with her.

"What did you say?" Mother fell down on the couch, "Get your mother a cool cloth baby and hurry. I feel a faint comin' on."

I scurried to the bathroom and grabbed a thick white washcloth and ran it under the freezing faucet getting it back to mother before she passed out. I wouldn't be able to hide her when Harry got here. She's the very last person that needs to be here when he arrives. Then I realized I had no idea when he was getting into town. I had so much to do-- like just wake up and get dressed. Then it occurred to me. Harry had never seen me this pregnant. He had left for D.C. over two months ago, and I had done a lot of, err... blossoming since then. The bottom line was that I needed

Kitty out and now.

"Here you go, Mother. Now come on. I have to get dressed."

"Is that jackass coming here? Oh, Blake, please tell me he's not coming here." I knew if I told her the truth, she'd stay. In fact, she'd order popcorn for the show plus knives to throw at him. So I fibbed—a little.

"No, Mother. I'm gonna meet him and hear what he has to say. That's all."

"Well, make sure y'all aren't in public. That paparazzi will be swarming all over that man like flies on shit and I don't want my baby, let alone my grandbaby, anywhere near the stink."

"Mother, I'm a big girl. I love you but I'll be just fine. Now come on. I'll help you up. You need to run by Krispy Kreme and check on Nanny. I know she was coughing when I checked in on her last night."

I held out my hand to help her up and kept the conversation focused on Meridee.

"Did she see the news last night?" I asked. "Harry has no idea he's flying right into the hornets' nest."

"She saw it. That's why she called me over. I stopped by with some spaghetti from DePalma's. It's her favorite, but she didn't eat much and was coughing a lot. She may be coming down with something. So I'll go check in and call you tonight."

Kitty wiggled her rotund rear out the front door, still holding the cloth to her temple. She was a little on the dramatic side but a good mother. Despite how different we were, I knew I would always need my mother, like any real southern girl. I just didn't need her here *right now*.

I kissed her goodbye and stood in the doorway watching her drive away. It was sunny out but still freezing, the bare trees cracking as the cold air swirled. The tall pines to the back of the little dirt road smelled of lush evergreen and the fragrance found my nose.

I loved the seasons. It helped me mark time and bring back memories. I loved my sensual memories of evenings underneath a twilight sky, or a soft breeze that kissed my cheek in summer, or the crunch of fall leaves beneath my feet on a crisp fall day. Tuscaloosa had great seasons. Well, except for dog breath season, my name for the heat of summer in the Deep South. The air feels like a big dog breathing on your face with one big, long exhale.

Seasons are earthy and as a mother, I now felt so connected to earth and time and life. Motherhood was already changing me, slowing me down to be present and in the moments. And, this moment was fixin' to be a doozy.

I made my way to the shower with plans to call Vivi. I had just stepped under the hot water when the rapping picked up again at the front door. What the hell, I thought. It's like a fiesta of Avon Ladies at the door today. I grabbed my robe pulling it around my still damp body. The banging continued as I walked through the bedroom and back into the front room. I could see a man through the beveled glass. It was Harry. On so many levels, I was really not ready for him.

CHAPTER 6

I yelled through the door to him. Harry was antsy, a mass of color and shadow shifting his weight looking like he was a bundle of nerves. I could see his image as though in a funhouse mirror through the beveled edges of the front door glass.

"Harry?" I shouted, "just a minute, okay? I gotta get dressed."

"Blake, it's not like I haven't seen you before. I'm freezing. Just open the door and I'll close my eyes. Come on!" He was begging—using persuasion like the top-notch attorney he was.

I exhaled giving in and flung open the door. The chill hit me like a deep freeze, especially since I was still wet from the shower. Harry stepped inside brushing past me in my big white towel around my huge pregnant stomach.

"Whew, thanks," he said as he stepped into the living room, his dress shoes clicking on the hardwood floor of Sonny's big lodge styled craftsman. He was in his dark overcoat and clutching a brown leather duffle in his gloved hand. He was GQ from head to toe. I always loved that look.

Harry stopped in his tracks, released his bag and stared at my belly, his gaze dropping the minute he was inside, the door clicking shut behind him. His blue-gray eyes found their way back to mine; a half smile crept across his lips. I looked back at him and suddenly felt my stomach drop like when you're on a carnival ride. For some reason, I felt nervous-- Harry standing there, me wrapped in a towel, my dark long hair damp and clinging to my bare shoulders. I could see a genuineness glistening in his eyes for the first time in years. I knew deep down he felt bad—for all that really bad behavior that broke up our marriage. He looked sorry and happy for me all at the same time. I wanted to believe what I saw, though the logical attorney in me shouted warnings.

There was a moment when we were both silent, looking at each other, then he reached over to hug me. I was caught in that moment of sensing his joy for me. I leaned in to him and my thick white towel suddenly fell to the floor. I stood before him, nude and very pregnant. I realized Harry had probably never seen a pregnant woman naked before. His mouth dropped open as he bent quickly to grab my towel. I embarrassingly tried to cover my huge self with the palms of my hands placed over the strategic netherlands.

"Oh my God, Blake, I'm so sorry," he awkwardly apologized.

"Oh Lord! Give me that thing!" I snatched the towel from him and wrapped myself, scurrying back to the bedroom, my bare bottom waving goodbye as I went.

"Well, you look the same from behind," he laughed.

"Very funny. Have a seat. I'll be right back." I actually felt better after the towel fell. Maybe I knew I had nothing to hide. I was all out there—in every way. The laughter broke the awkwardness. I mean, really, what could we do now? Everything was suddenly real.

I pulled on my soft navy yoga pants with the built in pregnancy waist and slipped a simple white t-shirt over my head. It covered my belly since it belonged to Sonny. The shirt still held his cologne with a whiff of his signature peppermint gum. It was like I was taking Sonny with me to talk to Harry. It was my suit of armor, subconsciously of course.

"Harry, can I get you something to drink? Coffee, some orange juice?" I said hurrying out to get this over-with. The elephant in the room was there and this time it wasn't me. It was the intern.

"No," he said from the couch, "maybe just a gin and tonic."

"Harry, it's not even 8 AM!"

"For me it's nearly 9 AM. I've been up all night. Never went to bed, so actually it's basically midnight and I need a drink, a real drink."

His cuff links on his stiff white dress shirt caught the early morning light streaming in from the front windows, flashing rays into the hallway. The sudden flicker darted up the wall and pulled me back to a time when those cuff links had made me swoon. I had loved how perfect Harry always was on the outside. It was the messy inside that was always the problem.

I grabbed myself a club soda and made Harry his gin and tonic from Sonny's bar near the stone fireplace in the main room. I handed Harry his drink then sat down near him in on oversized leather chair. I wondered if I should play dumb and let Harry put on this little act he had cooked up, or get right to it. The bad girl got the better of me. I decided to let Harry gravel a bit before we talked about his antics with the intern.

"Harry, what can I do for you?" I started the discussion

like a business meeting, waiting to see what direction he was going. He had told me yesterday that he still loved me.

"Blake, I know I did a lot of bad things. I just want you to know I'm really sorry. I was so stupid, you know, just caught up in the run for office. I meant what I said yesterday…"

I interrupted him. "What Harry? What did you say?" I wanted to watch his face when he said it--see him in person--see if he squirmed. I knew all of his looks and body language by heart. He could never fool me.

"You know-- what I told you yesterday on the phone. I meant it." He wiggled out of it.

"What are you talking about?" I asked pushing him.

"Blake, come on. You know what I said."

"You said so many things, Harry. Which thing are you talking about?"

"Blake, Listen to me. This is not a joke to me."

He brought his gaze up to my face, and amazingly, looked me straight in the eyes nervously. He inhaled and exhaled deeply, then continued.

"What I said yesterday is true. I …I... well, I still love you."

Then it was my turn to inhale. Wow! There it was. He said it again and he looked honest. But I knew what all the media were reporting. I couldn't hold back any longer. He was making me mad now. How could he say he loved me while he was all over TV cavorting with his twenty-year-old college student intern? I dove in.

"Love? Hmm, Harry I don't know. Did you tell your intern you loved her too?"

He was visibly startled. He stood up and fidgeted, straightening his tie, throwing his head back with a swig of his gin and tonic. "Ahem," he cleared his throat. "I know that's what's out there now. It just …it really isn't true. I was…I, uhm, I was set up."

"Oh for God's sake, Harry, you gotta be kiddin' me. Set up? Now that's a stretch even for you." I was shocked at his explanation. "Seriously, who in the world could be after you—let alone why in the world would someone be after you?"

"I know, but it's true. I mean--this girl was a set-up. She was sent to me to throw me off." He kept digging his own grave, right there in the living room.

"Harry," I shook my head and began to laugh. "Seriously just stop. I saw the paper yesterday and it was on the news at six o'clock last night too. Pictures don't lie. You did what you did. Everybody in Tuscaloosa now knows it. In fact, it's not even smart for you to be here. Your constituents are going to be calling for your resignation just like they did Clinton's."

"But the difference is I never had sex with her."

"Yeah well, Billy boy said the very same thing."

"No, I mean I never was even naked with her." He was still digging.

I smirked at him and furrowed my brows. "Come on, please. You and I both know the clothes don't have to come off. A dress? A cigar perhaps? Maybe sex, maybe not."

"Blake, I swear. I need to clear my name and you are the best at that. You've been a genius with Vivi's problems over the years. Plus what I said is true. I mean-- the divorce will be final soon, and I still love you. I do."

"Harry, look. I know if you are in the middle of reconciling with me, the intern story might lose its power. You're using me for your own gain, just like you did last summer when we pretended to still be in love to get you elected. I'm not helping you again. What we had once was really good for a long time; and frankly, I find this little plea of yours quite disgusting. Also degrading."

"No Blake…" I cut him off heaving myself up out of my chair.

"Stop right there. I've heard enough. You know I had high hopes for you. At one time you were such a wonderful man, Harry. Now you want to hide behind me to make the public believe we are reconciling? You're doing all this to try to cover up the fling with your sleazy little tart? That is an all time low, even for you. Now I need you to leave before you cause this baby to make an early arrival."

"Blake, I don't even have a car. I took a cab here."

"I'll call one for you," I said grabbing my cell and making the appointment for Harry to be picked up.

"You can stand on the porch while you wait." I pointed to the door as he hung his head moving back across the wooden floor.

"I'm sorry you made such a mess of your life, Harry, but I'm really happy. I can't be a part of your incredible disasters anymore. I can't continue to cover for you. If you could just keep little peter in your pants, your might reach your potential."

"I'm sorry Blake. I'm sorry for hurting you. I'm sorry I came here. I-- just…I still mean it and I always will whether you believe it or not. That intern and I never shared anything more than that one kiss and the media ran wild with it. You have my word."

"And we know what that's worth," I shot back. "Goodbye Harry."

He slowly stepped outside into the chilly morning air as I hurriedly closed the door behind him. I hung my head in both anger and sadness, for him mostly. He really started out as a different man. Or had he been different? Maybe I never saw the real Harry. Maybe I had refused to see it. But I knew in that moment I had witnessed the unraveling of a brilliant lawyer and senator. It made me so sad.

Harry stood just on the other side of the door, waiting for his ride. I stood inside, my back against the cold beveled glass. We were on opposite sides, divided physically by thin pieces of glass and wood, but miles apart in how we had both moved on. Here I was on top of my world with Sonny and the baby coming and Harry was in a free fall from his perch atop the Capitol. God help us as I realized the mere inches that actually separated us. He could, in a heartbeat, take me right down with him.

CHAPTER 7

I pulled into Vivi's, my tires spitting gravel as I quickly came to a stop in front of the rose gardens, now dormant for the winter. I slid out of the warm leather seat of my little black BMW, having had the intoxicating seat heaters on full blast all the way. My backside was toasty warm as I made my way around the front of the car and walked to the base of the front steps. Vivi stepped out onto the wide front porch of her old plantation house, drying her hands on her apron.

"Hey honey! Get yer ass on in here outta this cold. Did you know they've predicted an ice storm this weekend? I miss the milder winters we used to have. What in hell is going on? Alabama gettin' snow now nearly every year? Don't make no sense to me." Vivi was as warm and genuine as always, never worried one minute about what she said. She was in black leggings and a long crimson sweater setting off her copper wiry curls that framed her pale freckled face.

I smiled and waddled up the stairs, in through the formal dining room and back to Vivi's huge oak kitchen table. Tallulah was in her bassinette asleep in the butler's pantry near the back door. The TV was on in the corner of the counter top with some Hollywood entertainment show. It was on for background noise and maybe company. The warm room was splashed in a buttery yellow glow, a combination of the paint on the walls and the soft light of early morning dancing through the trees out the window. The house smelled like apple pies and hot cider. Vivi was nesting. And it suited her.

"Sit down, Honey and tell me everything," she said poring cider into red ceramic cups with white snowflakes etched on the outside.

"Even in all this chaos, that damn fool swears he still loves me—and get this-- swears he didn't sleep with that intern." I took a sip of the warmed mulled liquid, swallowing slowly on purpose. I was soothing myself.

"He'll say whatever it takes to get what he needs. You know that," she said.

"I know it but he really looked sad, you know. I think he's scared."

"Of course he is! He may be thrown out of office before he's barely even sworn in!"

"He said something else that really threw me though." I shifted my weight.

"What?"

"He said it was a set-up. That someone was out to get him." I saw Vivi's face curl in utter doubt and near embarrassment for Harry.

"Blake," she shook her head as she talked, "he has really outdone himself this time. Now he's invented a boogieman. God, where will that man get off the Looney train?"

"What if he's telling the truth?" I pondered.

"Blake Elizabeth O'Hara Heart! There is no way

anybody forced him to lip lock with that little hussy. We all saw the pictures. They were splashed from TV to newspaper. You're just in a crazed state of pregnancy hormones. Now snap out of it."

I laughed. She was probably right. But that look in Harry's eyes stayed with me, hovering like a ghost in my head.

I sat with her catching up in the cozy warmth till our laughter finally woke precious Tallulah. Vivi was quick to get to her, but so calm and easy. She brought baby Tallulah to the table and sat with her, the baby nestling her little red head in the crook of her mother's neck. Both of them were perfectly content.

"You're such a natural at motherhood," I said. "I hope I will be too."

"You'll be the best. You were raised by one of the best. Even though that Kitty is nuts, she was sure a good momma to you. And hey, if Dallas can turn into a good mother, you certainly can handle it."

Dallas Dubois had at one time been my stepsister then we became life-long archenemies. But a few weeks back before Christmas, she fell in love, directed the Christmas play. Love seemed to do amazing things to her because she reached out to become friends with Vivi and me. She also found herself in the throws of her own maternal instincts with a little girl from the Christmas play. Sara Grace Griffin was a foster child that Dallas took in over the entire holiday period and now she had filed papers to adopt her.

Dallas is also pretty cozied up to Cal, Lewis' best friend. Cal is a gorgeous University of Alabama professor and former quarterback for the Crimson Tide. Dallas, the local TV anchor, is a busty, leggy blonde who pretty much looks perfect all the time. I would have to hate her if I hadn't decided to be friends with her. Underneath all that blonde hair was a girl with spunk and substance. Meridee always liked her and now I can see why myself.

"I know it. I'm happy for Dallas though. I'm praying everyday that the adoption with that little Sara Grace goes through like a dream. Those two need each other," I said as I got up to pour Vivi and me a fresh cup.

"Yeah, and Sara Grace is already in elementary school and those sweet little older babies are so hard to adopt too. Plus, now that Dallas is engaged to Cal, they're gonna make one gorgeous family. I think they're already plannin' the wedding."

"I just worry, you know?" I said.

"About what, Honey?" Vivi suddenly looked concerned. I don't usually let anyone know my vulnerabilities. I've always been the strong one. Vivi leaned on me, not the other way around.

"What I'm gonna do." I shared with Vivi my anxiety. "I mean, is it normal to be like this? I don't know how I'll juggle the law practice and the baby. Part of me wants to stay home, play and teach this baby and just love on him all day long," I said looking down at my tummy and rubbing it. "But the other part me shouts, *what in the world did you suffer through law school for if you just stay home?* I mean I don't know if I can do all of it."

"Listen to me, Blake. Those women who told us we could have it all were tellin' a partial lie, you know?"

"What do you mean?"

"Well, they preached like a Baptist minister on Sunday—*We are women here us roar, we can have it all,* right? Well the secret is-- we can-- just not all at one time."

"That still doesn't help. How am I gonna know which to do, stay home or keep my practice?"

"Sweetie, you'll know. I was so scared too. I had no idea if I even had the mother instinct-- remember that talk we had before I got married? I was scared shitless. But you know what? The minute that baby was here, my inner momma bear kicked in and nothing would stand in my way. The little secret is so easy and you have more of it in high doses than you even know what to do with."

"Really? What is it?" I suddenly felt like a child finding out the secret of Santa Claus.

"Love, sweetheart. Just love," she said smiling sweetly. "It will act as a guide and it is never wrong. And I promise, when you get that baby boy in your arms, you'll know."

I let that float around in my head for a minute, my eyes stinging now with salty tears. I knew she was right, but the weeks before the baby comes were sure stressful. I remember Vivi, reading every book out there then shouting, "*I have no idea what this is even talking about!*" Then she'd throw the book down on the table in anxiety-filled huff. Now I knew just how she felt.

Suddenly the back door flung wide open and Bonita appeared. "Hey ladies! Y'all hungry for lunch? We got it ready to go and I saw your car up here Blake? How's my little mama?" She stretched across the table to give me a big Bonita hug.

"She's a nervous wreck," Vivi answered for me. "But I just got Tallulah back to sleep and I'm starved."

"Good. Arthur wants to bring it up himself. Says he hadn't seen his Blake in far too long and so he'll be up here in a jiffy," she said with a smile. She turned her ample hips with a grin and headed back into the cold.

Arthur was wonderful and his new BBQ business was fixin' to franchise all over town. The Moonwinx was a dream of his and he dove right in, with Bonita Baldwin by his side. Arthur was older, in his middle 50s and of African American descent. He had always been the gardener but at Christmastime, Vivi discovered he was her blood cousin and the real owner of the plantation. He deeded it back to Vivi for Christmas but she gave him back all the property for his business. So now, they were pretty much co-owners of the entire property.

Arthur was Vivi's only family and she was his too. They had always been each other's. Vivi's dad had died and her mother spent much of Vivi's young life in and out of institutions. She was very sickly all of Vivi's life. I have always been Vivi's sister—well since she and I decided we would be sisters from the first day we met in third grade at St. Catherine's Catholic School. And in eighth grade we created The Sassy Belles with our other good friend, Rhonda Cartwright. But she moved away that summer. Vivi and I are still Sassy Belles to the inth degree.

Bonita is a plus-sized African American doll, and we just loved her from the get-go. We made her a Sassy Belle right away when she and Arthur got serious. She was still the assistant homicide investigator and worked full-time with Sonny but I knew in my heart she was madly in love with Arthur and I told Sonny she'd quit before we knew it to help Arthur build that business if he needed her.

"My, heavens above! Let me see that!" I shouted, grabbing her hand and bringing it under my face.

"When did this happen?"

"Yeah, when were you gonna tell *me*?" Vivi looked hurt and left out. Arthur was her only family and she felt entitled to be the first to know.

"It just happened last night. We were gonna tell y'all tonight. Arthur was so cute. I just love that man like nobody's business," Bonita gleamed.

"Well, honey I am so happy for y'all! Vivi jumped up and threw her arms around Bonita's neck.

"Thank y'all, I am totally over the moon!" Bonita had a permanent grin stretched across her beautiful face. "I said yes, in case you couldn't tell." She threw her head back and laughed a deep rolling laugh as she waved her hand around like a movie star.

She and Arthur were great together. And their BBQ was quickly becoming legendary. Especially on game days and cold Saturdays. People were lining up all the way down the plantation drive to get those succulent ribs and heavenly peach cobbler.

Bonita stuck her head back in the door, "Blake, Sonny got some news today and he just called my cell. He's been trying to reach you all morning."

"Damn, I guess I left my cell in the car."

"I'll go get it. You need to just stay put," Vivi said. "Watch Tallulah for me."

"What's going on?" I asked Bonita.

"You'll never guess where that old man had been. You know that one Sonny's been investigating that was found dead at the wheel of his car the other night?"

"Yeah, where?"

"Seems like he had been playing strip poker with a hooker out at the trailer park."

"The trailer park?

"Yeah. Seems like somebody out there's runnin' a good old fashioned brothel."

CHAPTER 8

"Look what the cat dragged in," Vivi announced as she entered the kitchen from going out to my car for the cell phone.

Kitty and Meridee, my mother and grandmother were right behind Vivi. Meridee was pretty much the matriarch of everyone in my little circle. Meridee was a tiny little spitfire who had just turned eighty years old last summer. She had thrown herself a Hollywood nights themed party complete with half naked cowboys carrying her in on a Persian cot. That tells a person a lot about my Meridee. This tiny woman was the center of my universe when I was little.

"Hey y'all. How my girls doin' on this cold winter day?" Meridee asked reaching to hug me as she entered the warm kitchen.

"I'm good," I said still thinking about the news Bonita just shot out there. It was no secret, Myra Jean; the Trailer Park Psychic lived out at the trailer park where Sonny and Bonita made their discovery. And Meridee had been friends with her for as long as I could remember. I needed to talk to

Sonny but not now, not in front of Meridee. Lord knows she'd call Myra Jean and then Miss Myra would get the whole trailer park all in an uproar. I had no choice but I had to wait. Plus, Kitty was known as the town crier so nothing was safe around her.

"Hey Baby", Kitty said snagging a grape from a ceramic bowl of fruit near the corner TV. "You get Vivi up to speed on that ass of a husband of yours?"

"Yes, Mother and he's pretty much not my husband anymore."

"Well, legally he is and I don't want your name dragged across the mud with his. Hell, there's already a petition circulating to get that man kicked out of office,"

We all looked at her.

"For real, y'all. I just heard it at Krispy Kreme. Everybody was chatting about it."

"You mean you got Krispy Kremes in that car and you didn't even bring them in?" Vivi jumped in.

"Were they *Hot Now*? What were you thinkin'?"

"Okay Okay, I'll share. If I have to." Kitty pouted then turned to head back outside to get the warm sweet fried confections.

"Meridee, what are you and Kitty doin' out together today?" I asked.

Meridee looked down and then away. I instantly felt my stomach drop. "Is something wrong?" I asked.

"Oh you know that crazy mother of yours. She keeps dragging me to doctors for checkups. She's got the craziest ideas that I need regular check-ups."

Kitty came through the dining room door with the Krispy Kremes just as I heard the catch in her voice. I detected something. My eyes darted over to Vivi just as her eyes grabbed mine from across the table. It didn't feel right.

"Mother, y'all been at the doctor this morning?" I threw

it out there. I wanted to get a look at Kitty. She was the very worst at keeping anything a secret.

"Yeah, that old woman is so damn difficult. I told her she's not a spring chicken anymore and maybe we need a check-up. Finally I convinced her."

But I wasn't totally convinced. About it being just a check-up. I quickly looked at Vivi again and she looked concerned too.

"Just a check-up huh?" Vivi pushed.

"Oh, Yeah. You know, just making sure everything's still in the right place. Now give me one of those doughnuts. I'm starved."

"She had to fast for all the blood work so I know she's hungry." Kitty just let the cat out.

"What do you mean? Blood work? Why?" I was getting anxious.

"It's nothing," Meridee said biting into the sweetness. "I'm just fine. Kitty is just insistent that I get my blood done and all that since I'm so *old*." She smiled as she chewed, trying to keep us from getting too upset. Making like it was no big deal. But I felt a twist in my stomach.

"I finally got her there by promising to take her to see Dr. Riley."

"He's a stud, I'll say. Hard from head to toe," Meridee took another bite grinning because she loved shocking us.

"Meridee!" Vivi shouted turning as red as her mop top. "I wanna be like Meridee when I'm eighty." Vivi was giggling as she got up to get the plates for Bonita and Arthurs BBQ that was on the way.

"No one's gonna be hungry if we eat all these right now. Arthur's on his way up here with lunch. Y'all stay okay?" Vivi told them more than she was asking. Meridee jumped up and grabbed some silverware and helped Vivi.

"I need to run out and make a call," I said. "Be right

back."

"Honey, you can call from here. It's cold outside." Kitty suggested.

"Oh, uhm… sometimes my cell doesn't pick up from inside." I slipped through the dining room and out to the front porch to call Sonny. The cold air slapped my warm cheeks as I hit his picture on my cell.

"Hey, baby. Forget your cell?"

"Yeah, sorry. So there's a real life brothel? I can't even believe that."

"Yep. You never know. We found a phone number on the dead body of that old guy and traced it. Turns out he was just leaving an appointment from somewhere out there. We think we know which trailer it is too. Doesn't that psychic Vivi saw for her bridal shower live out there?"

"Yes but why?" I asked. Did you wanna talk to her? I can't imagine she'd know the hookers."

"Come on Blake, she's a psychic right? I mean doesn't she know everything?"

CHAPTER 9

I drove home after lunch in deep thought, Harry at the top of my mind. It was all so confusing. I knew him better than most and something about that look he gave me when I threw him out earlier that morning bothered me. I wanted to know for sure. Harry said someone set him up, but the picture was of him kissing that brunette. That was a certainty. Maybe he was just full of it like always, using whatever woman would get him to the top.

I pulled in to the drive at Sonny's. Well it was my home too, now. I had to get used to that. My old antebellum dream house I shared with Harry sat across town near campus empty and dark. I kept swearing I was gonna put it up for sale but somehow I just never really get around to it.

I went inside and my curiosity got the better of me. I went straight to my laptop.

I'm a lawyer, a researcher, so I knew if anyone could dig up the truth, I could do it. I got out the newspaper and looked at the picture of the intern in a lip-lock with my soon-to-be-ex. Her name was included in the article and her hometown. Jessica Jamison. Twenty years old from South Carolina. Interning in D.C. for the semester. Wow! She sure doesn't waist any time, I thought. I decided to dig a little deeper.

A few more clicks of the keys led me to another clue about this aggressive little intern. She has relatives here in Tuscaloosa. I decided I needed to find out exactly whom she's related to and maybe go knock on their door. Then I stopped myself.

Why? Why in the world am I putting myself through this to help Harry? I caught him with two different women last summer as our marriage was ending. And in spite of all that he still counted on me to stand by him and help him get elected. Am I a fool?

I got up to search the fridge for something to drink when I heard the doorbell. I turned and hurried back to the door.

"Hey honey, get in here. It's freezing out there," I said reaching in and pulling Vivi inside. "What are you doing here?"

"I just talked to Lewis and he found out some stuff about that intern," she said stepping inside and taking off her olive green wool overcoat. Her cream cashmere scarf set her red hair and ruby lips off like a portrait. "I left the baby with Arthur but I gotta be back in an hour so he can get the dinner shift going. Now listen, Harry's in deeper trouble with this little affair. Looks like he may not get to stay in office if Tuscaloosa has a thing to say about it."

"How do you know?"

"Lewis just had a visitor at the radio station."

"Who? And why does it matter?"

"Well, Lewis said that petition has snowballed with support in just a matter of hours. All it took was that picture of that lusty little hussy kissing Harry and Tuscaloosa wants him out. Now."

"So who was at the radio station today?"

"That freakin' used car salesman, would be politico, Bullhorn McGraw."

"That idiot that ran against Harry? What the hell did he want?"

"He bought an add."

"For what, his old car lot?"

"No, honey. He's telling everyone to get Harry outta Washington and send him instead."

"Harry hasn't even been pushed out yet."

"Well, it may not be long."

I handed Vivi a cup of hot chocolate from the microwave and threw in a couple of mini marshmallows. I sipped the chocolaty silk and it warmed me—but only for the second it took to slide down my throat. Just then, someone began knocking on the front door. Vivi and I were both leaning on the kitchen counter cups in hand when we were startled by the noise.

"God, this place is grand central today. I'll be right back." I said as I sat my warm cup down next to Vivi's and headed down the hallway to the front room. I could see a tall blonde through the beveled glass.

"Hey Dallas. My goodness, what a surprise!"

"Hey Blake, how are you doing these days?"

"Good," I said a little curiously. "Come on in. Vivi and I were just having some hot chocolate. Can I get you some?"

"Yeah," she sighed. "Can I leave my coat here?"

Dallas removed her creamy white long wool coat and laid it over the leather chair in the corner, tossing her crimson velvet gloves on top of the coat. I felt like a whale near the spiked high-heeled, centerfold like TV anchor.

"Hey Dallas," Vivi said as we entered the kitchen.

"Whadja think of that story on Harry last night?" Leave it to Vivi to get the conversation started.

"I know it. It was unreal. It's the top story line for the day—probably for the rest of the month with that petition going around. Really that's one of the reasons I'm here."

"Really?" I said handing Dallas her hot chocolate, my confusion just continuing to grow.

"Yeah, I saw all the pictures in the news and I even tried to call Harry all day long. I never got him. Only his voicemail and he never has called me back."

"He's in hiding, I'm sure," Vivi said swigging her hot chocolate.

"Well, I for one believe he might be innocent." Dallas said, looking at both of us like she had a secret. Suddenly she had our complete attention. Vivi and I set our red ceramic cups down on the granite counter-tops in unison, our mouths dropped open like fish gasping for water.

"What? What do you know?" I asked her leaning left toward the end of the center island.

"Sonny's working that dead body case right? The one with the old man slumped over?"

"Yeah. He found a number and an address that led him to the trailer park. But what does that have to do with Harry?"

"Well, I got a tip into the newsroom this morning about Harry. It was from a resident of River Pines. The trailer park."

"What the hell?" Vivi pushed.

Dallas curled her long blonde hair behind her ear and shifted her weight from one hip to another. Then she set her cup down next to mine, leaning in as if no one else should hear.

"I think Harry could be telling the truth. There's reason to believe he may have been set up."

"Can you share anything about this tip? I mean I know all about confidentiality." I was prying, but technically we're still talking about my husband. The divorce was supposed to be final soon. Plus the baby was coming. Not that my new little sweetheart had anything to do with it. I knew he would choose his own time to arrive without deferral to any of us to make his debut into this world. But, still the birth did involve me and it was on my mind. I knew I had to get this whole mess with Harry solved before I was pushing this new little life into this world. I had an agenda.

"You know, I'd tell you if I could," Dallas said. "But listen to me. I need proof to blow this story wide open. Something tells me the three of us can do it. Blake, you know how to dig through certain records, Vivi you can help us keep an eye on Harry through Lewis and please, if anything crazy happens at the radio station, let us know."

"Am I hearing this plan right?" Vivi folded her arms and huffed with a slight eye roll.

"What do you mean?" Dallas seemed insulted.

"The three of us are fixin' to become sleuths—together—to clear Harry Heart, your soon-to-be-ex husband; Dallas' ex-lover; and my ass of a brother-in-law?"

Dallas and I looked at each other and exchanged wry smiles and nodded together. It really was unbelievable.

"Looks like you've summed it all up." I said shaking my head in disbelief after hearing the plan put into real words.

"Okay," Vivi agreed, "as long I got it straight, I'm in."

The three of us each picked up our cups of now cooled hot chocolate and toasted.

"To Harry," I said. "May we get his ass back to Washington!"

CHAPTER 10

Later that evening the house was quiet—for a change. I had put a fire in the huge stone fireplace, lit candles on the mantle. I had left the pine greenery in place on the mantle; tiny white lights gleaming from beneath the long scented needles and pinecones.

Dinner was warming in the oven. The amber lights of Sonny's old craftsman home were aglow with the warmth and respite of a cold winter's night. I sat cuddled on the leather couch, in my fuzziest pink socks with a cream colored soft throw over me, my laptop open to dig a little more into the life of Harry's sexy little intern when Sonny walked through the door.

"Hey beautiful," he said grinning. He leaned down and kissed my lips, his so cold from the frigid night outside. His icy cheek brushed mine with his end-of-the-day whiskers. He was the sexiest man I had ever known. He stirred me like no one else. He could be standing clear across the room and my eyes catch his, his one eyebrow would raise and God, it was all I could do not to jump in right there in public. It had always been that way between us: Hot. Always.

"Hey handsome, how was your day? Anymore leads on that poor dead guy?"

"Well, we know who he is —or was. Why he was out at the newly discovered hen house so to speak has me stumped. I mean we know why he was there but there's no pattern there. He was a first-timer. And the number in his pocket was from a girl who recently became uhm… an employee there." He stopped and looked at my laptop. "What are you up to?"

I filled him in but wanted to keep quiet for now about me, Vivi and Dallas pulling a "Charlie's Angels" stunt with Harry. He might wonder why we all decided to be involved.

"Just working on a case for somebody," I blew it off.

"Smells good babe, what's cookin'?" he headed off to the kitchen, removing his gloves and scarf as he went.

"Yum, looks delicious," he said from the kitchen. "Hey there's three cups here in the sink, one covered in lots of red lipstick. Who was here today?"

Oh, Lord, I thought, why didn't I stick those cups in the dishwasher? I *know* why. I was intensely focused on the little hussy. And when I'm focused, God, help us all.

Just then I heard my cell. Literally saved by the bell. "Just a minute baby, I can't hear you," I yelled toward the kitchen.

"Hello?" I answered.

"Hey Blake, this is Dallas."

"Oh, hey, any news?" I asked anxiously.

"Yeah, at least I think so. You know you said you thought the intern was related to someone here in Tuscaloosa?"

"Yeah?" I answered with heightened interest.

"I think I may have a lead here. Seems like she had a job in town before she got that internship. I am trying to tie it down and see where she might have worked—you know—how long she had worked there and all that. There may be some information that could be a lead."

"Wow, that's awesome. What can I do from here?"

"Just keep looking into her work life. I think it may be our best hope."

"Will do and keep me posted. This is great."

"I will. And Uhm…Blake, I need a little advice. Maybe a favor."

I sat still. I had no idea Dallas, even though we had recently become friends after years of being in the arch nemesis category, would ever admit she needed me for anything. I mean she asked me to help her with the broken set at the Christmas play last month but a favor? I was interested for sure.

"No problem," I said. "What's going on?"

"I'm really nervous about this adoption. Sara Grace is really counting on it all and I'll just die if I can't give her a home." She suddenly became emotional. I could hear her voice quake as she spoke.

"Sure, let me figure out what we can do. I know people on the board and so does Meridee. Maybe we can come up with something. What is the delay?"

"Well, they didn't come out and say it but since they are delaying, I think they don't like that I'm single. Cal and I are engaged but my relationship to Sara Grace is just between her and me. I don't want Cal to feel like he *has* to marry me now, you know?"

"No, but that is what you would want, right?"

"Well, I do, secretly, but it needs to be his idea. I mean we are engaged and all but I don't want him to feel rushed because of the adoption. We haven't even set a date yet." Dallas' voice was trembling. I knew she loved the little girl so much. Sara Grace lost her mother last year and her father had been absent her whole life. No one had come forward for her so she wound up in the system.

"Anything else, I mean about Sara Grace? Is there nobody else in the picture?"

She paused. I could hear her breathing and felt the worst was coming.

"I know her mother and father are both gone. And I don't think there's anyone else close to her or that even lives here in town."

"But if there is a blood relative, that person may be trying to get her as well, or the agency could be having trouble locating them to get them to sign some documents. Let me check into it and I'll get back to you as soon as I can."

"Oh, Blake, that's wonderful."

"No biggie," I assured her.

"No, Blake, it is. I mean…she has become my whole world. I--I love her. She needs me and I need her." Her voice quaked again. There was really so much more to Dallas than I ever gave her credit for.

"It'll be okay," I said. "I'll call you tomorrow."

I hung up and heaved myself off the couch and went to find Sonny in the kitchen. I now had an answer for those cups in the sink.

"Sorry, honey. What were you saying?" I asked as I entered the kitchen.

"Who was that?" he asked licking the icing off a cupcake.

"That was Dallas. She just had a question."

"Oh, is that who was here earlier with all that lipstick?" He motioned to the stained cup in the sink.

"Yeah, she stopped by. Vivi was over too." The detective in him could sometimes be irritating.

"Whatch'all cookin' up these days?" He joked winking

at me.

He walked over to the drawers and got out some red checked mitten potholders. He put them on and opened the oven door and pulled out my lasagna. I knew he loved it so I made it and threw it in before I started researching again. Sonny was great like that. He would come in and see what needed to be done and just jump in and do it. I knew he was gonna make a wonderful daddy. His mood was light and he just seemed happy—joyful, from someplace deep inside. I stopped and reminded myself to be in this moment, watching him dart around the kitchen, dishtowel slung over his shoulder, setting the table over near the bay window. The light was dim and the moonlight streamed in through the back windows, first dancing through the pine trees that covered the backyard, the cool blue shadows then splashing across the walls of the old farm styled kitchen.

Sonny grabbed little silver candleholders and opened another drawer to pick out two white taper candles and the lighter. Before I knew it, our kitchen looked like a little Italian Bistro. All we needed was the melody of a violin and an accordion.

"May I seat you my princess?" God I loved this man. They broke the mold when they made him. I took my seat and he filled my champagne glass with water, keeping our little sweetheart safe. Drinking and eating healthy for the baby was my first concern. I had been perfect; even gave up my diet coke for the entire term. But as soon as baby was here, a good margarita was in order.

"Thank you baby. You are quite the host." I winked at him. I knew times like these would be rare soon.

"You are quite welcome, gorgeous. I'm just so glad I get to come home to you. All my dreams have already come true. He's the icing on the cake." Sonny's eyes were glistening as he referred to our baby growing inside me. "I could never want for anything else."

I smiled at him and lifted my glass in a toast.

"To us, and our new little family," he offered.

I couldn't speak. A lump formed in my throat as I grinned, tears in my eyes. I clanked his glass as the candlelight flickered, Sonny's deep brown eyes sparkling as he looked at me. Both of us knew. Our new little bundle would change things. In a good way of course but things would be different nonetheless. And Sonny and I had just gotten started. We had been waiting since we were barely fourteen years old to finally make love and be together. It all finally had happened this summer and before we knew it, our baby was on the way, as my marriage to Harry was dissolving right in front of me. Harry was out of control, his campaign occupying his every moment, except the one afternoon when I caught him putting his clothes back on—I caught him just as he was putting his pants back on after an afternoon delight with judge Jane Shamblin. Yep, I said judge.

All in the past--now Sonny and I were so excited about the baby coming. It was a boy. His boy. And it was all we could think about. Until Harry flew in today.

Sonny and I finished dinner and slipped into the living room with some warm cider. The fire was still ablaze and inviting us in for the cozy evening ahead. I was more than ready to be held and cuddled by my man.

"Come sit with me, babe. I need to love on my girl," Sonny said patting the seat of the couch near the heavy soft pile of blankets. Just as he plopped down we heard a muffled "Hail To The Chief" coming from inside the couch.

"What in holy hell is that? He yelped."

"I have no earthly idea!" I bent over and started digging next to Sonny down into the seat cracks. The song played again. There was no mistaking it, Hail To The Chief.

"Here it is," I announced, pulling out some strange cell phone.

"Who the hell does that belong to?" Sonny asked looking at the number causing the phone to ring.

"This must be Harry's phone. He was sitting right here when he dropped by this morning.

"He always was an ambitious son-of-a-gun." Sonny laughed, "Hail To The Chief." He sure had plans to take this career of his a tad beyond the senate seat he's trying to hang onto." Sonny studied the now silent phone.

Then…

"Good God almighty!"

"What?"

"The number. I recognize this number calling Harry."

"Who is it?"

Sonny was quiet. Like he wasn't sure he should say. Like it could be that awful. Then he just hung his head. "I'm sure there must be an explanation."

"What Sonny! What? Who is calling Harry?"

"The phone call is coming from that trailer park brothel."

CHAPTER 11

There was certainly no sleeping after that. I tossed and turned all night wondering where Harry was and what the hell he was up to. And most importantly, was I a total fool for giving him the benefit of the doubt? When I woke up I knew I had to get to Vivi. She'd at least know the answer to the question. And she'd say, "He's an ass. Always has been. Always will be." Maybe it was just what I needed to hear so we could all drop this case and get back to our own lives.

Vivi met me for lunch at the City Café in Northport just over the river from downtown Tuscaloosa. We both loved that place. In college I think we ate there three days a week at least. Nowhere else can you get a meat and three for so cheap. It's unreal! And of course, my very favorite southern dish served in heaping helpings-- fried green tomatoes.

The age-old rusty sign on the covered sidewalk invited us inside the warm, sprawling but cramped interior. It was a weird layout. And you had to keep looking for a table. It wasn't a first-come-first-serve type place as much as it was a first-come- first-spot establishment. If you spotted a table, you'd better get to it. People stood in line every single day for this place that served just plain ol' good country cookin'. All of us crowded up near the front screened door that slammed when you walked inside. The little hole in the wall spread out sideways to the left, into other rooms, all jammed with tables and Formica-topped booths and the friendliest waitresses you ever met. It just felt good to be in out of the winter chill and be served comfort food with a smile.

"Let's grab that table, quick," Vivi pushed. But my pregnant ass could not maneuver through the hoards of townsfolk. "Well, we lost that one," Vivi huffed at me. "Look, I'll go ahead of you and grab the next one I see. You do your best to get through to me."

I felt like we were in a huddle and I needed to clap. Okay, she had a plan. The fresh cornbread and soft buttermilk biscuits were calling her name.

"Okay," she announced. "Here I go."

It was like she was heading in to the deep forest with her bow arched like a huntress.

"I got one," she yelled. "Come on."

And suddenly I was trapped between a lady with a walker and the fat man from the circus. There was no slipping through. It was gonna have to be like a football play, straight up the middle. Only one problem, I needed blocking. Vivi saw I was in trouble and like the offensive line, she showed up to block.

" 'Scuse me, pregnant lady, comin' through. 'Scuse me y'all, pregnant lady."

Great, thank you BFF for life. I am now the most embarrassed pregnant lady. Ever.

"Thank you sweetheart, I have no idea what I would do without you," I smiled as I sat at the table she'd saved. "Remind me the next time we're lookin' for a town crier."

Vivi and I ordered the meat and three. In the South,

that's a chicken breast, a hamburger steak, or a "meat" and the three are the sides, like mashed potatoes, or boiled cabbage or in my case, three orders of fried green tomatoes.

By the time I told Vivi all about the phone call from the brothel we were knee- deep in cornbread.

"I just can't believe you still think he could be telling you the truth. I mean that he was set up—not to mention that he said he still loves you. I mean for God's sake, Blake. Really?"

I let out a huge sigh and leaned back in my chair resting my folded hands on my big belly. "I know the whole thing doesn't make a bit of sense in a logical form but my gut tells me to keep looking."

"That is exactly what makes you such a great lawyer. You rely on your gut even more than that brilliant logical mind. But I still have one teensy little problem with all this do-goodin' we're doin tryin' to help Harry. He told you he still loves you." She stopped eating and put her fork down with a clank, her eyebrows up at me. Still chewing she wiped her mouth, never once taking her eyes off me. I knew she was right. And she knew I knew it, too. Harry was using me.

I mean it was a problem. Harry saying he still loved me—using his love for me as his alibi. Then followed by the big news over his indiscretion. But the last bit of what he said to me was what lingered. "I've been set up, Blake," he said, just before I threw him out the door. It began to gnaw at me because of the way he looked at me when he said it. I had known Harry Heart for over fifteen years and knew every look he had. And something told me he really believed he was set up. I just had a need to know the truth. It was my nature.

"I know but maybe with all this going on he was just feeling emotional. I have decided to overlook that part of all this. He said he was set up and my instincts just tell me to see if maybe he might be telling the truth."

"Well, that would be a big deal for him."

"What, him still loving me?"

"No, him telling the truth."

We both laughed. I loved knowing I would always have Vivi in my corner. We had been together through thick and thin for nearly our entire lives. Usually it was me saving her from some God-awful misunderstanding but today, I felt more like I needed her just a tad more than she needed me.

"Do you have any idea where he is?" I asked her.

"No. Lewis said he hasn't seen him since yesterday morning. Harry came out to the radio station just as the news was breaking. Lewis said he shoved him into his office and shut the door. Reporters were everywhere."

"We need to find him. I have a ton of questions. The problem is, I have his phone so I can't call him," I said.

"He's bound to be looking for it," Vivi reasoned.

"I just wonder where he's hiding out. There're not a lot of places our newly elected senator can hide in his hometown." I was thinking out loud as I took a swig of my tea.

"Well, I wonder an even bigger question, *who* is he hiding out with?"

"I can't imagine he would even take that chance." Then I wondered myself.

"Well, why do you think he got that call from that brothel?"

"No idea. But it sure doesn't look good for him." I started trying to piece it all together in my mind.

"Well, that needs to be the very next thing we work on," Vivi suggested. "We have to find him. Maybe Dallas has some ideas on that. She's pretty good at sniffing out a story, maybe she can dig him up. I'll give her a call this afternoon."

"And I'm gonna see what all I can find out about this brothel. I mean can you believe it—a brothel? Right here in Tuscaloosa?"

The waitress brought us our dessert of homemade banana pudding and both of us dug right in like we were still starving. I had a thought that if I could just stay right here and rest between meals, I could have dinner, then sleep till lunch tomorrow. Then eat again all right here from the table. Nice idea if I weren't solving a sex scandal of my soon to be ex, and oh yeah, fixin' to have my first baby with my one true lover, the homicide detective. My life suddenly seemed like a three ring circus. Usually it was Vivi's life that was the circus. Just then, I heard my phone in my purse. It was Kitty.

"Hey Mother. Vivi and I are out to lunch," I answered.

"Blake, sweetie," her voice was cracking.

"What? What mother? What's wrong?"

I could see the sudden worry in Vivi's eyes.

"Oh, God. Okay, We'll be right there." I hung up and dropped the phone in my purse as I pushed back from the table. I looked up at Vivi and told her.

"It's Meridee. She's collapsed."

"Let's go." Vivi jumped up and helped me to the car.

CHAPTER 12

Vivi and I rushed into the emergency room of Druid City Hospital.

"Where is she?" I asked a nurse as we approached the triage desk. The stark white walls were cold and un-nerving. Kitty was walking out of a room to the side of the desk just as we entered.

"That old woman has finally scared me half to death. I swear, next time it will be both of us here in the ER."

I could tell she was covering with sarcasm, a family trait. Tears pooled in her bright blue eyes as she reached to hug me, a little tighter and a little longer than usual. I knew she was scared. I was too.

"Mother, what happened?" I asked as she let go of me and reached to hug Vivi.

"We were on our way to the grocery store. I really don't like her to drive anymore. She could barely see over the steering wheel as it was and now her eyesight is questionable most of the time. So I was turning there near the bakery at Fifteenth Street and Hargrove and she just fell over into the door, slumped sideways. I pulled over and when I couldn't get her to open her eyes I called the ambulance."

"What are they saying?" Vivi asked wanting the details.

"They have taken her to do some tests."

"Is she conscious?"

"Yeah, but kinda confused."

All of us looked at each other, our faces washed in a veil of worry. The love for our matriarch was too much to even describe. Meridee had practically raised Vivi since Vivi's own mother had been so sick most of her life. Meridee was "mother" to all of us, our men included. Vivi and Mother and I walked over to the uncomfortable chairs in the waiting room. Vivi sat next to me and reached over and placed her hand on mine with a squeeze.

"She's gonna be fine. I just know it," she said looking straight into my eyes. Vivi was trying to soothe us as best she could. She gave Kitty and me a reassuring smile as she patted Kitty's knee and nodded. I knew she was as worried as we were. "Come on y'all, we know what a stubborn Sassy Belle she is. She's not going anywhere." As we sat together holding each other up, waiting for word from Meridee's doctor, I heard the automatic sliding doors open bursting in a blast of the chilly air. I looked up and felt my heart jump. It was Sonny. My knight in shining armor.

"Hey baby," he said bending down to hold me. I stood up and rested in his arms. His jacket was still cold and his cheeks were rosy. But I could feel his warm hands rubbing my back and I felt like everything was gonna be okay. Sonny had a way of doing that. If he were there, it would all be taken care of. He was commanding at well over six feet tall and had an in-charge type of presence with his broad shoulders and large build. He was protective. He held me for a minute then I felt one of his hands let go. I glanced to my left and he was holding Kitty with his other hand.

"I got here as soon as I heard," he said. "Is she okay?"

Meridee had raised all of us. As a teenager, when Sonny and I were "on again" he was at her house as much as I was. And Kitty had always loved him too. He had been family to us since I was fourteen years old and it just felt so good to have him right there for all of us.

"We're waiting to hear from her doctor," I answered. "They have her back doing tests right now. Who called you? I was so upset all I could think of was to get here in a hurry. I was gonna call as soon as we knew something."

Kitty looked up at me and smiled, a tear falling from her cheek. "I called him right after I called you. I knew we all needed him here with us." She squeezed his hand.

Lewis came running in from the parking lot and Vivi stood up with her arms out. Lewis hugged her tight as I saw tears form in Vivi's green eyes. It was like now that her own knight was here she could let down a minute and the worry just flowed. We were all so scared.

Just as we all sat back down the doctor came through the double doors. We all stood in unison. His face was neutral. I tried to read him but he looked stoic and all business. My heart raced a little faster as I squeezed Sonny's hand looking at the doctor as he approached us.

"Okay she's resting comfortably in her room now," Dr. Allen announced.

"Well, what did the tests show?" Kitty asked, her voice shaky with nerves. We were all anxious and impatient.

"She's had a stroke."

Vivi and I dropped our mouths open as our men held us a little tighter. Kitty gasped, her hand over her mouth.

"It was what we call a TIA, or mini-stroke. She may have been having these for a while now and not even have realized it. Today's might have been a bit stronger."

"Can she still talk, or walk?"

"Yes, she's okay. The mini strokes don't debilitate the way massive strokes do. She should be her normal self. It can make her a bit confused so be patient with her. I'm putting her on some medication but she'll need to be watched as we work to get all the dosages just right."

"Is she gonna be okay? I mean, is this a forewarning of some kind?" Sonny spoke for all of us.

"She should be fine. People can live with TIAs for years," Dr. Allen reassured us. "For a woman of eighty years old, I'd say other than that she's in pretty great shape, but we're gonna keep an eye on her."

"Oh, thank you so much," Kitty leaned in to hug the good doctor. A sense of relief washed over the tense mood of our little group. That was until that blast of cold air hit us when the automatic double doors opened again—and in walked Harry.

CHAPTER 13

"Good God, now I think *I'm* gonna have a stroke."
Kitty clutched her pearls and for a minute I thought she was
either gonna fall over or yank them from her neck and
strangle Harry with them. I totally went into shock. The
lawyer in me kicked in with all the questions. Where had he
been? Who had he been staying with all this time? And what
the hell was that brothel doing calling his phone? Not to
mention, how did he know we were all here?

"What are you doing here?" The first question jumped
from my lips before I could put my tongue in control.

"How is she?" Harry asked.

"She's gonna be fine. A stroke," I said unconsciously
folding my arms.

"Oh, my God! A stroke?" Harry seemed fidgety.
Nervous-- but not exactly because of Meridee. I could tell
he knew he was in shark-infested waters between all of us
standing there together. Little did he know that Vivi and I
had committed with Dallas to try to untangle him from his
latest web of trouble.

"Yeah but Dr. Allen is handling her and he has her on some prescriptions. We're all gonna watch her. Where have you been? I know you didn't have a car."

Harry shifted his weight, his face flushed with the cold outside and maybe a bit of awkwardness. "Uhm, well, I can't really say. I was wondering though if maybe you ran across my phone. I can't find it anywhere."

"Yeah, I have it in my purse," I said walking back over to the chairs to grab it for him. "I couldn't call you, since you obviously don't have your phone," I sneered. I got his phone from my black leather Michael Kors tote and handed Harry his phone, but not before pointing out his latest call.

"Here it is," I said holding up the device. "But I was wondering if you could explain this number. Whomever it is has called several times since last night."

Harry took the phone and studied the number. His mouth dropped in a confused look. I wasn't sure if it was fake or not. Then he shook his head.

"That number started calling me just before I hired the intern," he responded. "I answered it one time and they said it was a wrong number. But for some reason they continue to call from time to time. I usually just ignore it."

Well, that was pretty good, I thought to myself. He was still as fast as he always was in court. An expert with quickness like nobody else. Why oh why did I have this nagging feeling that he just might be telling me the truth. I hated that. I wanted to hate him. To at least be mad at him. He had been a notorious liar all summer long. Maybe it was the pregnancy hormones. Carrying Sonny's baby boy made it hard to hate anyone. Ugh, a part of me just wanted to shove Harry right back out into the cold parking lot of the hospital, but instead somehow I felt sorry for him. He was fast becoming such an outcast, right here in his old hometown. Not to mention right here among the people that were once his family.

Lewis walked over and patted Harry's back. "Thanks for coming, how in the world did you hear about Meridee?"

I had to admit, I was still wondering that myself.

"Well, here and there," he hem-hawed.

Just then the doctor interrupted. "Y'all can go on in and see her if you want. I just checked on her and she wants to know –and I quote—"if any damn body out here cares about the old lady."

"Okay why don't you three go on in and we'll all wait out here," Sonny motioned to me and Kitty and Vivi as he rested his hand in the small of my back. I could feel his body next to mine now and it relaxed me in the chaos. For a moment, I forgot about Harry.

Vivi nodded to me, "Let's get in there now."

"Yeah, I got a few things to say to her myself," Kitty winked at me and inhaled a deep breath of relief. The three of us headed into Meridee's room not even thinking what we might see. None of us were prepared to see my lively vibrant grandmother lying in the hospital bed, tubes running in and out of her. A knot formed in my throat.

"Oh, Blake, Oh, baby, come over here and give me a hug," Meridee whispered.

"Old lady, you scared me half to death," Kitty said her voice trembling.

"Nanny, my Lord, what are you trying to do to us? You really didn't need to go to all this trouble to get some attention. You know we love you." I was joking with her and got a funny little grin.

"Yeah, I mean really-- all this?" Vivi played along motioning around the room at the machines keeping track of her vitals.

"Well, I was wondering if y'all were gonna stay out there and party without me," Meridee joked. She looked more frail lying there in that bed than I could ever remember. My heart was full. I loved that tiny woman more than life and I wanted her here to hold the life that was growing inside me. I felt in that moment, watching the room glow with the love of all the women in my life, that I was only a tiny part of the chain. From Meridee to Kitty to Vivi and me and now to mine and Vivi's babies, we are all forever linked—reaching back into the past with one hand while our other rests gently on the future. I rubbed my baby belly as a gush of happiness filled me. I knew in that second Meridee was gonna be okay to see my boy.

"Where are those men of y'all's? Kitty I know that mayor of yours can't be too far away."

"Hey ladies, did I hear somebody mention a mayor?" Charley Wynn, Tuscaloosa mayor and Kitty's fiancé stuck his head in with a big grin. He was big, kinda round and reminded me of Jeff Bridges. Kitty rushed over and hugged him. He kissed her head and Kitty exhaled for the first time in an hour. He would be number five, as in husbands, for Kitty. But I thought maybe this one might stick. They seemed really in love. I could do worse than having the mayor for a stepdad.

"Hey, we're gonna need to get in here for a second," Sonny rushed into Meridee's room and shut the door. He had Harry by the arm. "The media is here. Somebody from inside the hospital must've let the cat outta the bag. They all know Harry's here. I had to get him outta the waiting room."

"My God, Harry. It's just not safe for you to be anywhere these days," Vivi jumped in. No sooner had we gotten Harry in the room and everybody calmed, then a sudden knock came from the door. Kitty opened it without thinking as Dallas rushed in. Thank God, she was alone, her long-time cameraman, Daniel nowhere in sight.

"Y'all, I thought we were gonna make sure to keep each other in the loop," she said with her hands on her hips, her long bouncy blonde hair falling over her winter-white suit.

"We had no idea, Harry just showed up here without any warning," I explained.

"Well, somebody had to tell him Meridee was here," Dallas reasoned.

"So true, and all of us are in the dark here about who called him and just where he's been staying. Not to mention the brothel calls." Now I had my hands on my hips, frustrated with all the secrecy.

"Brothel?" Dallas said in shock. "You mean he has something to do with all that talk we been hearing about there being a secret brothel in town?"

Harry stood quietly as he inched toward the door.

"What are y'all talking about?" Meridee perked up.

"It's okay, Nanny. Harry is just here for a few days to clear some things up. He's been staying somewhere in town and we were just talking to him about where he's been." I was trying to include her without being too overwhelming. I knew even though the doctor said the TIAs weren't debilitating, I understood she was tired and maybe still a tad confused. Weren't we all!

Meridee spoke up, loud and clear. "Well, I can tell y'all one thing—Harry sure as hell hadn't been staying at no brothel—he's been stayin' with me."

CHAPTER 15

"Oh, good God almighty! Is that the houseguest we were grocery shoppin' for when you passed out earlier?" Kitty jumped in.

"Well, he *is* a houseguest since he is stayin' with me," Meridee explained.

"Where the hell has he been? I've been in and out of your house several times in the last couple of days and I never saw him."

"That was the plan. I needed to help him stay outta site till this whole mess blows over."

Okay clearly she wasn't as confused as I thought. She was flat out nuts.

"Mother, you can't hide a fugitive!" Kitty exploded. "I mean there's a petition to get him out of office. He's trouble right now. That's probably why you started havin' these TMJ's—all the stress. Harry, how could you do this to her?"

I shook my head and jumped in. "Mother! It's not TMJ's—surely there's nothing wrong with her jaw or her speech. They're TIAs and you're right-- no wonder she's been so stressed! Harry you should be ashamed taking her up on her offer."

Then, it occurred to me that second that of course Meridee would take him in. That's what she always does. She finds the misunderstood, the underdogs and fights for them. She had helped Lewis open his radio station. She always defended Dallas even when the rest of us hated her; she saw something good in her. Meridee had a nose for the deep down truth and somehow she must have known Harry was telling the truth.

"How did you get here?" I pushed him for answers.

"I took cab. I was at Meridee's when the phone rang. The caller ID announced the hospital so I answered and was told she had been brought in. I told them I was her next of kin."

Lying came so easy for him.

Harry just stood there, head down, propped against the wall. "I'm sorry," he said. "I just wanted to come home to tell Blake before the news hit about Jessica. None of it's even true," he pleaded, "I swear."

"We all need to get out of this room now and let Ms. Meridee get her rest," Sonny took charge. "Come on y'all, we'll sneak out the back to my squad car and get Harry back to safety away from those paparazzi out there." Sonny looked at me and gave me a nod. I knew he was right. We needed to go. The room was too crowded and Meridee wanted to believe she was her same ol' normal self. So she'd push to make it all good with Harry. We needed to leave right that second or she could over do it.

"I love you, Nanny. We got this, okay. You rest. We're gonna need you as soon as you can get home. This baby boy needs his great Nanny." I patted my tummy smiling, then leaned over her and kissed her little cheek. She was such a tiny woman, all five feet of her and maybe a hundred and ten pounds soaking wet. "I love you."

"I love you too," she responded. "Now y'all be careful." She laid her little gray head back on her pillows.

"You just drive me crazy," Kitty said bending over her bed to kiss Meridee's cheek. I'm not going anywhere old woman. I wanna stay right here till I can take you home." She turned to Mayor Charlie and me. "They said they're gonna watch her overnight, and I can just sleep here in her room."

"Ill keep watch over both of y'all as long as they'll let me stay," the mayor said sweetly, patting Mother's shoulder.

Sonny led Harry out through the swarm of reporters and then in through the hospital where the reporters weren't allowed. Vivi and I stepped toward the hall, Dallas moved over to Nanny's bedside. I saw Nanny reach over and squeeze her hand.

"Don't you worry, sweetheart. I called the children's home this morning and they said they were sure they could get that paperwork on your baby girl pushed through. They are just as anxious to get Sara Grace to you, as you are to get her. They said she's been askin' for you every single day."

"Oh, Miss Meridee, you are an angel. Can I go see her?"

"Sure you can. You can call them and ask for a visit. I'm sure they would love to have you."

Dallas leaned down and kissed Meridee's cheek. "Thank you so much. How can I ever repay you for helping me?"

"Don't you go a worryin' 'bout that. We all just take care of each other. We're family." Meridee smiled and inhaled a deep breath. It made her feel good to help people. It was evident all over her face.

I took that in for a moment. Meridee truly was an angel. I just didn't want heaven to be her address just yet. I had so much more to learn from her. How could I ever be such a good judge of character? And so smart when it comes to people? She was our sun, the center of our family universe. Nope she wasn't going anywhere. My baby boy needed to know this amazing little woman.

"We need to have a quick chat," Dallas said as she made her way back to Vivi and me near the door.

"As long as it's private for now," Vivi offered. "No big news story."

"No problem, but when we get this thing figured out, I want an exclusive," Dallas proposed.

"Deal," I said.

We headed through the throng of microphones just behind Sonny and Harry. Vivi tippy-toed up and kissed Lewis on the cheek.

"I'll stay here and keep everyone occupied with some sort of rhetoric till y'all let me know you're safely out," Lewis promised. He was always good at running block for his team as a former Alabama football star and great with the microphone as The Crimson Tide's football announcer. He would be in his element with the reporters keeping them busy till we escaped with Harry. Lewis winked at us as we went through the double doors leading to the rest of the hospital.

Vivi and Dallas and I arrived at the back maintenance doors where Sonny had moved his unmarked car.

"Okay, Dallas, come with us to my house and we'll all have a chat with Harry," Vivi ordered. "Maybe we'll all get some answers tonight."

CHAPTER 15

It kinda felt like we were kidnapping Harry. Everyone had questions for him and images danced in my head of us tying him down till he talked. I knew of course it wouldn't really be like that but I liked seeing it that way.

Sonny and Harry sat in the front seat while the three of us would-be sleuths sat together in the back. Sonny drove us all home to Vivi's for a nice little chat with Harry. It was time to get his full story if any of us were gonna even begin to solve this mess.

Between the brothel and Harry's scandal, we had what's called an A news day going on and Dallas would have the lead story for the rest of the week at this rate. Even though she got the anchor job, they wanted to keep her out front doing a few stories a week. And her getting an up close exclusive with the scandalous senator was quite the coo for her new seat at the anchor desk.

"Come on inside y'all. I'll get some hot cider and coffee goin,'" Vivi said as we made our way inside her warm, comfortable, old plantation house. It had been in

Vivi's family for well over a hundred and fifty years. The light outside was growing dim, the bare trees blanketed in a lavender haze as the sun was setting. It slipped into the horizon so early on these midwinter days.

We all found a seat around the huge oak table. Vivi got everything going, set some chocolate chip cookies out and excused herself to see her precious bundle. Her new sitter, Misty, had stayed with Tallulah while we had been gone.

"Harry, I have a few questions and we need a straight answer," Sonny began, not messing around with jovial small talk. "I'm not here to delve into your personal life or the debacle it's become. I'm not here to judge you either. I need to know what you know about this brothel."

"Sonny, honest to God, I don't know anything. That number has been calling me for a month. I never even knew it was anything but a wrong number." Harry suddenly seemed like a child.

"Sonny, I have been searching for answers about this case too for the news," Dallas interrupted, "and I know the man you found dead in his car had just had an appointment there. He had seen a woman named Jasmine. Not that she's the same woman that is Harry's intern. But upon further investigation, Harry's intern does have ties to Tuscaloosa. I think she may even have an uncle here."

"How does this tie together? What are you thinking?" Sonny asked her.

"I found a vital piece of information on Jasmine today. She isn't originally from here either but she too has an uncle here. I have a source out at that brothel."

"I've already talked to her trying to learn more about the dead guy. She was more than likely the last one to see him alive. Now we need to get more information from her. I mean it's a real stretch—lots of people have uncles here," Sonny said.

Harry sat there looking uncomfortable. "I do remember something," he perked up.

"What? About the brothel?" I asked.

"No about my intern. Her name is Jessica but she wanted everyone on staff to call her Jaz. Said it was a nickname from her childhood."

"Was she from here?" Sonny asked.

"Yeah," Harry said suddenly sitting up straight in his chair. "I mean she was in school here. That was the whole reason I wanted her on my team. She was a hometown girl. I'm not sure if she's actually from here originally, but she said she was a student at the University."

"Okay, I think we know what we need to do," Dallas pitched. "We need to find out everything we can about both of these young women. Maybe they're related."

I was still not drawing the correlation—at least not enough to make a complete case. "Harry, tell us everything you know about your intern. Most importantly I need to know what makes you think you were set up?"

I sat waiting, hungry to prove to myself I wasn't a total fool for trying to help him.

"I just know."

That was it. I was waiting for the big reveal and that was all he could give me. Behavior like a third-grader—"Just 'cause." I shook my head.

"Harry, look. We're trying to help you. You have to tell us everything. I mean come on—you're a lawyer. You know we need to know everything."

"Okay, but really it was just nothing. I mean I hired her just a few weeks ago, right after I got to Washington to start setting up my new staff. I needed a personal intern and she applied. I had my assistant interview everyone and I told him to pay close attention to anyone from Tuscaloosa or even with strong ties here. Jessica made the cut and I interviewed her. She was charming and warm and seemed very capable. So I hired her."

"But how did all these pictures come up?" I kept pushing.

"I couldn't figure it out myself," he said. "But every single time she was with me, a photographer happened to be there. The second she saw them she'd kiss me on the cheek. Over the last few weeks it became a nuisance. I'd walk out of my office and she'd offer to assist me wherever I was going, and before I knew it we were being followed by a camera-man or two.

I thought it strange to be so loved by the press already, but I liked the publicity. Come to think of it, maybe they took that picture on my birthday when my new staff celebrated my birthday with a cake. I think she did kiss me during that little celebration in my office, and of course, someone had a camera there to capture the event. Yes, that was the first time she kissed me on the mouth with a photographer present. She gave me a kiss and I remember she whispered how excited she was to be working for me. I think she kinda idolized me."

"Yeah, uh huh," I smirked. I looked at Harry. Clearly he did love all that attention. He was in the right place as our senator. That was for sure. He loved the limelight, like a Kennedy. And he was great at his job too. He had such a love for his constituents, and for his hometown. He and I did have that in common.

"Finally, last week, we had a press conference," he continued. "I had been answering questions when a certain photographer suddenly showed up in the crowd. I had seen him over and over in the weeks before. He always seemed to be in the crowd. Then before I knew it, Jessica grabbed me and kissed me on the lips again. The photographers went wild. After it was over I told her she'd have to leave. None of this would be good."

"Hell, that's an understatement," Vivi hissed as she joined us with the baby on her hip. It broke the testimony as she brought the baby in for a visit.

"Look at that precious little girl—she looks so much like you, Vivi," I cooed reaching up to kiss baby Tallulah's little foot. Baby's feet are so adorable. Those little fat feet, I could just eat 'em up. I couldn't wait for my little sweetheart to get here.

I could see Harry's face warm to her. He hadn't seen her at all until this moment. By the time she was born he had already left Tuscaloosa for D.C. He grinned at the little girl. All of us saw him, his face flushed. This was his niece after all, Lewis' baby girl.

Vivi bent down to him sitting at the table. "Wanna hold her, Harry? You missed the birth and the christening. She's your very own flesh and blood ya know? Let me introduce you to your niece, Miss Tallulah Heart." Vivi smiled proudly.

Sonny and I watched from the opposite side of the table, Harry reaching up to take the little pink bundle from Vivi's arms. I felt Sonny's big warm hand slide over my knee and his fingers clutch my hand. I looked up at him and smiled. It was an awkward moment in a way as Harry and I hadn't signed the final papers for our divorce yet. I looked at him but he was lost in the moment, holding his new niece in his arms. I knew in my heart he was telling the truth about the intern.

"That baby is just gorgeous," Dallas declared. Vivi you and Lewis have to be so proud. I so hope I will be having a daughter soon, too."

"Oh, really?" Vivi inquired. "Is there something you aren't telling us?"

Dallas laughed, "Oh, no. I'm not giving birth to a baby.

But I am trying to become a mother. Sara Grace was my daughter for nearly four weeks at Christmas and I need her back with me. I'm trying to adopt her."

Harry looked up. He seemed shocked. Dallas had changed after he left town. So much had happened since he left and he was just starting to see how we all had moved on without him.

"Well congratulations, Dallas. That's wonderful news." Harry finally spoke up.

"Thanks, Harry."

"And don't forget to tell Harry who the new man in your life is." Vivi kept right on making things uncomfortable. It was one of her specialties.

"Yes, Well, I'm seeing Cal these days. We're engaged."

"Cal? Cal Hollingsworth? Our old Bama quarterback?"

"One and the same," Dallas smiled a bit embarrassed. I knew Vivi all too well and she was trying to make a point. We all had grown up and it was time Harry did the same.

"Yeah, I love Cal. Things are going great for us but with my baby girl, I'm stuck in limbo right now. Seems like there might be a hold-up or something. These things usually take more than a few months. Anyway they're working on it at the Children's Home. Any word yet?" She suddenly directed herself to me.

"No, uhm-- I haven't heard back from anyone," I slid a half-truth in. The thing was I hadn't even had a chance to talk to anyone. Meridee knew everyone on the board and we did have Harlan McCullough the probate judge to pull some strings if he could. But it would probably take a little more time. I tried to encourage her anyway.

"Maybe we'll hear something this week. I'll see if I can keep digging for you."

As we all adored Tallulah, Dallas' cell phone rang in her Chanel knock off.

"Scuse me y'all—it's the station."

As Dallas talked on her phone, I kept thinking. One thing was still bothering me. Who in the world would want to set Harry up? And why?

I looked at Sonny. "I need to get back to the station for a late meeting," he said, pushing back his chair and closing his notepad. "We're gonna have to shut this brothel down ASAP ya know? We just need the proof of what they're doin' out there. I mean we *know* what they're doin', but it's bein' run out of somebody's trailer home. We have to prove their charging for sex before we can shut 'em down. I have a lead on it."

"Go get 'em baby. Home for supper?"

"Yep. I won't be too late." he kissed me as he stood up. "Come on Harry. I'll drop you off at Meridee's on the way. We need to keep you safe till we get this settled."

"Hell, I was better off in Washington," Harry said. "But I feel like I need to stay here until the truth comes out. I don't want it to look like I'm running from something."

Hmm. Integrity. It was a new look on Harry and I liked it.

Dallas threw her phone back in her bag and looked at all of us from the end of the table where she was sitting.

"Big news y'all. Seems like some amateur photographer just came into the station trying to sell us pictures of Harry-- with Jessica the intern. I think we've found our paparazzi."

CHAPTER 16

"Meet me at the Tutwiler," Sonny said when he called me. I was on my way home but he said it was urgent. He sounded excited so even though I was tired and anxious to get home, I drove straight to the gorgeous old historical hotel just south of downtown. I pulled into the valet parking and gave the gentleman my keys and made my way inside the grand old foyer. The sweeping staircase curved up to the right.

My eyes followed the stairs and standing at the top was my knight, Sonny, hands in his pockets, his feet crossed at the ankles as he leaned against the top of the railing. He was smoldering, his left eyebrow up and that come to me look heating up my body.

What was he doing here? He made his way down the stairs and reached for me.

"I just wanted it to feel like we were on a date, that's all. You know-- before the baby comes. This will be our last Valentines Day as a couple. From now on, we'll be a family. So I wanted this one to be special."

"Oh, baby. You are so sweet. I had planned to make you dinner tomorrow night."

"Or maybe you could just *be* dinner," he grinned. "So come into the restaurant and order anything you want."

"Okay, but lemme run to the restroom. You know me and this pregnancy bladder."

"I do. I'll go too, that way we won't be disturbed at all."

Sonny led the way down the creamy-colored opulent hallway toward the first floor of rooms. The gorgeous old tapestry carpet took me back to a time and place so simple and sweet when my mother, Kitty would bring us here once a month for the Sunday buffets. Sconce lighting lit the amber hallway. But just as we approached the bathrooms, Sonny stopped short.

"Looky here," he said bending down. Somebody lost their room key."

"Huh, should we take it back to the front desk?" I asked.

"Why don't we try it first?"

And before I knew it Sonny had put the key in a random door and flung it open.

"You first, beautiful," he offered as he invited me in holding his hand out.

I was confused but followed his lead. The room was filled with lit candles, rose petals on the bed, and a prime rib dinner waiting on the table by the huge window.

"What is this?" I asked.

"Dinner. I thought we could have some privacy," he said proud of his surprise, a sly grin on his luscious lips.

"Oh, Sonny, this is the best surprise I have ever had. But my things? I need my night things."

"Over there, my little princess." And to my total amazement, Sonny had packed me an overnight bag, with all my lotions and potions and make-up for the next day. And he got it all exactly as if I had packed myself.

"How did you know what all I would need?"

"I watch you, baby. And I know you."

I had never felt more special or more loved in my entire life. My heart was so full—real love just filling me up. My eyes brimming with tears as I looked at him, his sweet brown eyes glistened too as he looked deeply at me. I sat down on the edge of the bed and Sonny dropped to his knees in front of me. He held my hands, caressing them as he spoke. "I love you so much Blake, you have made me the happiest man in the world. I get to sleep right next to my dream-girl every night, and wake up to my angel in the sunrise. I can't believe my teenaged dreams all came true." He kissed me deeply.

I saw several gifts wrapped in red velvet and tied with white satin bows.

"You even brought me presents? Oh baby, I don't have my Valentine's gift here for you, sweetheart," I said walking my fingers up his suit coat and kissing his neck.

"Baby, you're the only gift I'll ever need." He kissed me softly with his warm lips, devouring me and pressing his hard body into mine.

We feasted on our decadent dinner then stretched out over the red silky rose petals on the huge king-sized bed. I had opened my presents of a silver necklace with a diamond studded heart dangling on it and a bracelet with one charm on it--baby booties.

"Whatcha thinkin, beautiful?" Sonny was lying next to me, the moonlight dancing over the heavy yellow and white quilts. The bed was so warm and next to Sonny's big muscled frame, my tired pregnant body finally relaxed.

"Just so much on my mind," I said snuggling into him. I was so happy just feeling his body next to mine. There was a definite difference between how I felt being with Harry and Sonny. When I was married to Harry, okay well, I still *am* but only technically, I knew I loved him. I felt a partnership with him. I used to think that was the most important thing—to be partners, interested in the same thing. Harry and I built our law practice based on this belief. But with Sonny, I've learned something about myself.

I now see how important it is to just feel safe and loved. The partnership thing is important, but what I love about being with Sonny is that constant feeling of being wrapped in love all the time. It has given me an unbelievable feeling of safety. I never felt so completely safe with anyone else. I have always felt this with him. I know if I'm next to him, I will always be okay. It's like I can slow down and just breathe. I don't have to perform. I can be in ratty sweats, cleaning the oven and he will sneak up behind me and suddenly I feel his warm lips on my neck. Harry never did that.

With Harry it was always how to get more, do more, make more and win. Eventually that just wasn't sexy. All that money and power was so empty. It was like our marriage was a mannequin—gorgeous, plastic --and without a soul.

With Sonny life was real and messy and spontaneous—and so very sexy.

My hands wandered down his toned thigh, slipping up to his warm hard manhood. I squeezed gently. He rolled over and kissed my ample round breasts. I could feel his hot breath on my skin. His hands travelled over my ass, cupping as he rolled his tongue over mine, kissing me deeply.

"Maybe I can give you something else to think about," he whispered as he licked my neck. Sonny and I never stopped being intimate the entire time I have been pregnant. And it was always wonderful and satisfying.

He slipped his hand inside my thighs and made his way inside, gently, as he kissed my neck. His lips dragged down my chest settling between my breasts. I opened myself to him lying on my side. Sonny loved me when I was sexy or even pregnant.

"God Blake, I don't think you've ever been more beautiful than you are right this minute." He kissed the mounds of each breast as he moved down.

"We are one inside you. Forever bonded in our love, is our son. I have never loved you more or found you more sexy than you are right now."

"I love you Sonny," I murmured, scratching my nails through his thick brown hair. I arched my head back letting him create his magic.

His warm wet tongue ran over my nipple as his hands turned me over and slid under the small of my back. He held himself up with his rippled muscular arms and entered me slowly then faster until we both fell into warm sweet ecstasy.

"I love you too, Blake." Sonny whispered as I sighed laying back.

I loved looking up at those sweet brown eyes, glistening in the candlelight; his hot sweaty body relaxed rolling over to lie next to me.

"No matter how old we get, no matter what life has planned for us, I love you. I have always loved you and will forever." He kissed my lips softly and held me in his arms.

We must have fallen asleep because the next thing I knew the sunrise had crept over our quilts, pushing aside the moonlight that had stretched over us just hours before. I turned to Sonny and snuggled up close to his warm, still sleeping body. Just as I was dozing back into slumber, I heard my cell ring. Please, I thought, it's only 6:30 am. It went to voicemail but instantly rang again.

I slipped from beneath Sonny's arm and out of the warm oasis to my purse over near the bay window.

"Hello? This better be good 'cause the sun isn't even up and I'm eight months pregnant."

"Blake, I'm sorry. It's Dallas. I just got a tip."

"Well, if it's not good, I have one for you too," I snapped.

"I just got a photo texted to me by an anonymous source. They blocked their number."

"What's the pic?"

"It looks like Jessica, the intern," she said still excited.

"Okay. We already know what she looks like. I don't get it."

"Well it's not just the photo of her; it's where she is that makes the difference."

"What? Is she in town?

"Oh, it looks like she's in town I do believe. We'll have to enhance the picture a bit but I'm pretty sure of where she is."

"Where? And it better be someplace other than Krispy Kreme."

"Blake, the picture is of Jessica coming out of that alleged brothel."

CHAPTER 17

"We're still waiting on lab results on that old guy I found slumped behind the wheel," Sonny said, sipping his hotel coffee in a rush as he gathered his things to head out the door. "If we get a positive on foul play then my department can get more involved. Since, I'm homicide, I may have to assist on this with Vice if the old guy died of natural causes."

I had informed him that Jessica may be here and doing something out at the trailer they're watching. But he really couldn't do much to help us with Harry. I knew that. Being homicide, Sonny would be limited, at least on a professional level, if Vice had to step in. I realized in that instant most of the work on the scandal with Harry would be done with me and my girl posse—Vivi and Dallas.

Sonny and I both had a lot to do today.

Our romantic getaway had ended too soon and we headed home, me following him as we drove. He helped me get my things inside.

"I'll check in with you later," I said tippy-toing up to

kiss him goodbye. "No matter what comes up today, I'll have happy thoughts after our wonderful Valentine's night."

He gave me a quick kiss and a hug. "Me too, baby—a night to remember forever," he grinned. "What's on tap for you today? I don't want you to do too much." He walked down the hallway to the front of the house to grab his coat.

"I'll be checking in on Mother and Meridee. I need to talk to Dallas too."

I followed him to see him out. My mind was already racing. If it were true that Jessica was in town, I wanted a word with her. I am still technically Harry's wife and all the pictures splashed across every form of media of her lips on my husband made me mad for some reason. Not because I was jealous, but because if Harry was right and she was up to something, I wanted her to know she had met her match. Me.

My mind swirled with ideas of what we could do to catch her. Sonny kissed my forehead and I shut the door behind him. Time for a plan. In seconds I was on the phone with Vivi.

I thought as I drove. And all I could think of was to stake out that brothel myself. I had a really good Nikon camera with a telephoto lens. Vivi and I could sit and watch and take pictures of the comings and goings in the trailer. Maybe we could even get inside. I mean with me being eight months and all, we might be noticeable. But we had to do something. If Jessica was there, I was bound and determined to find her.

"Get up here little mama and tell me all about it," Vivi motioned me inside the house from the gravel drive out front. "Tallulah's napping and Misty's on her way in case we need to leave. Dallas sent over the text of the girl leaving the trailer. She said she sent it to you too."

"Yeah, I got it," I said slipping off my red wool coat

and white gloves. "It's her, I'm sure. Lets upload it into your laptop and see if we can enhance it just so we get a good visual."

Vivi grabbed her laptop from the dining room table and brought it with us into the kitchen. Tallulah was in her warm crib in her cozy spot at the butler's pantry. We sat down and transferred the text to email and then uploaded it from there. Within minutes we had a clear shot.

"It is most definitely her." I said. "Let's call Dallas and see if they got the same image," I suggested.

"Okay. I know the TV station is gonna be on this story like flies on shit today but I thought of an idea that may get us inside that trailer," Vivi said.

I always loved Vivi's metaphors. If nothing else, they were certainly to the point. The second she said she had an idea I got nervous. I had a few ideas too but I was anxious to hear Vivi's plan first.

"Okay, before I call Dallas, let's hear it," I gulped. Vivi wiggled in her chair across the table from me. She leaned in toward me propping on the table and folded her hands together like she had a big secret.

"You know St. Catherine's is havin' that annual bake sale and clothin' drive right now? They're asking everybody to bring clothes and goodies to the church."

"You're not really suggesting we go sell cupcakes to the prostitutes and ask for them to donate their, uhm, used hooker clothes to the Catholic Church?" I paused for a second when she didn't answer. "Are you?" The look on her face told me everything. Vivi thought this would be a wonderful idea.

"Blake," she insisted, "hear me out."

"Okay, but just cause I need to laugh."

"Listen. We need to get inside. Us sittin' out there takin' pictures isn't enough. We need to prove that our little intern is doin' business. I mean my theory is that if she is an, uh, hmmm, employee of this establishment, someone who runs the place could have set her up—just like Harry's been saying."

"So you think if we offer cupcakes to all the hookers, they'll all rat on her—like icing is a truth serum?" I was baffled but when hearing a plan from Vivi this was usually the norm.

"No silly, though that does work with you—we'll go up to the door and knock and say we need clothes for the drive. We'll offer cupcakes. Then you say I really need to use your bathroom. Being so pregnant of course they'll understand and let you. We'll both have our phones and do what we can to gather some evidence. Sonny did say they needed evidence to shut the thing down. We'll be killin' two birds with one stone—helpin' Harry and helpin' Sonny. I think it's brilliant." Vivi leaned back in her chair smiling, obviously very satisfied with herself. I had to admit, it did sound interesting. I thought about it for a minute.

"How does this help us nab Jessica?" I wondered. "And besides how do we know she's behind the supposed set-up?"

"Well, that's where you're idea comes in. We sit and wait. When we see her go in, we go over and knock. We'll figure it out as we go."

"Okay, that's the part I don't like," I quipped. "I like a set plan."

"I know it Ms. Lawyer, but sometimes you gotta fly by the seat of your pants!"

"I think that is exactly how I landed myself into this little situation," I said patting my pregnant tummy, insinuating my early escapades with Sonny before I was totally divorced. Vivi threw her red mop of frizz back as she laughed at me.

"Touché, my dear, touché."

We had a plan in place. Vivi jumped up and threw a box recipe of cupcakes for us to sell in the oven. Whether this little sting would work or not we could only pray.

"I think we need to call Dallas and give her the tip that we're gonna try to get inside."

"Okay but we need to tell her to keep it quiet that it's us. That way if somehow we're able to pull this off we can just step aside and let Dallas and her microphone do what they do best."

I took in a deep breath. Were we really gonna do this? I just wanted the truth out there. And maybe—just maybe this would work. I must have been clouded with wanting the truth, cause I sure didn't see a problem at the time with going to a hooker house and asking for contributions to our fake Catholic clothing drive while we fed everybody cupcakes. But, I thought, here we go.

CHAPTER 18

Vivi called Misty to come in early and we got ready for our big steak-out. I left the Fru Fru's working on the removal of the hideous Vegas mural with a prayer that when I got home it would all seem like a nightmare. The nudes of Sonny and me would be gone and in its place I would have a beautiful baby blue and butter yellow nursery. I left them the keys and told them I'd be late and to lock it up. Fingers crossed no more naked parents or mythical creatures.

"I'm gonna pack us some water and snacks," Vivi announced. "Heaven only knows how long this is gonna take and we need to be prepared." She scurried around the kitchen gathering up supplies and packing them into a canvas bag.

Misty arrived, along with her " 'sup girl" boyfriend, Dax. He was dressed in an army jacket and combat boots. I was absolutely certain he had never been part of a battalion of any kind. He had a sweet smile though and his earring was nice. Make that earrings. Both of them. His backwards baseball cap covered a mop of brown curly hair. Both of them were staring at their phones and not looking up at each other or us until Vivi greeted them.

"Hey Ms. Heart. Thanks for letting me bring Dax. He just loves Tallulah," Misty offered. She was sweet, nicely dressed with pageant hair and lots of make-up. I couldn't see how they belonged together. I guess she liked the bad boys. It made me think for a minute though. Suddenly I wasn't sure how I could leave my new baby boy with anyone, especially all day long every day while I was at the office.

"Come on girlie, lets go," Vivi said hurrying the two of us out the door. "I'm not sure exactly when I'll be back, Misty. Arthur's just outside at the Moonwinx down the hill on the side yard. He said he's within earshot if you need him."

"Okay, y'all, don't worry 'bout a thing. We got this," Misty promised. Dax never spoke. I wasn't sure he could.

Vivi and I jumped into my black BMW armed with our food supply and headed out to River Pines, the infamous trailer park. Myra Jean the psychic lived there. I knew she had never seen my car so I wasn't worried she'd spot us. But I did begin to wonder if she had heard of any of the goings-on at this brothel.

We parked under a tree down near the river to set up watch over the cathouse. It was only ten o'clock in the morning. This was gonna be a long day. It was in the high forties but I was hot, having a hormonal tornado in my body. I took off my coat and gloves as Vivi and I sank down into our seats to be outta sight. Time crawled by. I drank an entire bottle of water and ate a whole bag of Doritos.

"I need to pee," I announced. Yep, I knew it would happen, but somehow when we made this little plan I wasn't thinking—I mean eight months pregnant, a water bottle and sitting in a car all afternoon might be kind of a bad plan.

"Well, we can't go in *now*, Vivi explained. "It'll blow our cover."

"What do you propose I do, then? I can't sit here in this condition."

"I know what," Vivi said with genuine excitement. "Why don't you go in this?" She then pulled out a Big Slurpee cup, a 32 ouncer from the floorboard.

"Are you kiddin' me? Do you recall that I am nearly at birth size for this baby? How in the world do you propose I position myself go in that little cup under my ass? In a car?"

"I know," she chided. "Get under here, no one will see you." Vivi reached over and grabbed a red fleece blanket I had folded in the backseat.

"Oh, so no one will notice a huge mound under a bright red blanket in the drivers seat of this car?"

"Well, you can't get out," she reasoned. It's broad daylight and there's only one tree out there. You'll be seen for sure. And you can't go inside the brothel. It's too early. They'll wonder why the pregnant lady is back sellin' cupcakes after just bein' there to pee. It will blow this whole plan. You sure don't wanna run over to Myra Jean's; she'll try doing a reading on the new baby. Look, I'll hold the blanket over you and when you're done you can just pour it right out the door. It's the only thing we can do for now."

"Ugh! How do I get into these situations?" I ranted. "Fine! Just hold the blanket." I gave in because if I didn't Vivi and I would be floating out of the car any minute. I pushed the automatic button and slid the camel leather seat backwards until it could go no further. I scooched to the back of my seat and pulled my legs up underneath me, attempting a squat with the big plastic cup between my legs. I unfortunately had on pants but they were the stretchy pregnancy pants. However, they were no easier to slide down than jeans for a lady with child. Plus, it was pitch dark under the blanket so I couldn't really tell what I was hitting when I put the cup in place. Not that I could see my crotch over my eight-month baby belly anyway. I prayed I was hitting the flimsy cup. Then,

"Oh No!" Vivi shouted. "Shit!"

Okay that is not what you wanna hear when your ass is hovering over a plastic cup mid-pee in the pitch dark while your   pregnant.

"What? What?" I shrieked in desperation from under the blanket.

"It's Miss Myra—she sees us."

"How do ya know?"

Hide quick! Slide down in the floor! She's waving her hand wildly as she drives over here." Vivi was frantic.

"No! No! No-- I'm not done. No! This is the embarrassment of my life!"

"Said the woman who was pregnant by another man while still married to our senator," Vivi snarked.

"Ha ha, this is no time for reminders. Please-- you gotta get rid of her."

"Okay," Vivi agreed, " but how do I explain this huge red blob in the front seat?"

"I don't know. Get out and greet her while I finish up," I urged. "Keep her from getting close to the car."

"Okay but I have no idea what I'm gonna say when she asks what's that huge red blanket covering—I'll just tell her to guess—she's the psychic."

I heard the door open and slam shut. In faint voices I could barely make out the muffled sounds of Vivi. "Hey Miss Myra, How're yew doin'?

"Hey there Miss Vivi," Myra chirped, "What in the world are you doing sittin' out here?"

"Oh, it was a lovely day so I brought me a picnic out here to the river," Vivi shot.

Good thinking Vivi, keep her occupied, I thought.

"All the way out here? I mean the trailer park is okay but wouldn't the Riverwalk have been better?" Myra was gonna be trouble.

"Good Lord have mercy, what the hell did you bring to your little outing? That is one massive picnic basket, I'll say. You must be really hungry or expecting an army."

I knew she spotted me under the red cover. I could hear her voice getting louder. Oh, no! She was approaching the car. Oh Lord. I was finished with my business but now I was trapped under the red fleece throw squatting while holding 32 ounces of piss. I just knew I was gonna wake up any minute. This had to be a nightmare.

I was still in my car seat squatting as Myra Jean opened the door to check out the oversized picnic basket that Vivi had supposedly brought to the river with her for her humungous picnic.

"Oh my goodness, this thing is huge," she boomed. I felt her hand grasp the coverlet at my shoulder and give it a yank. Then she yanked it again.

"How the hell do you have this thing tied up?" She pushed.

"No! I have it tied really secure so it wouldn't spill." Vivi kept explaining.

"Well, my God, this is some talented basket," she snipped.

"How do you mean?" Vivi questioned.

"Well, obviously it can drive. You have it tied down here in the driver's seat—behind the wheel."

I didn't hear anything else from Vivi.

One more huge yank from Myra and I began to teeter and lose my balance-- and my grip on my big warm cup. She gave one last heave and yanked the blanket off me like she was a magician and I was one big surprise, Voila—now here's me squatting on my car seat with my pants down, ass exposed with a big plastic Slurpee cup holding my pee.

"Lord have mercy! Blake! What the hell are you doin?" She yelled as I fell sideways and my pee then spilled over and out onto the cold ground outside, splashing her winter boots. Her velvet winter boots. The steam began to rise from the cold dirt.

"What the hell *is* that?" She bellowed.

"Well, Miss Myra, I was trying to have a moment of privacy."

She jumped backwards.

"You're not tellin' me this is…"

"Yep-- I sure am. I'm so sorry! I am so embarrassed. Let me help you," I said trying to un-squat and step out of my car pants still down. All my femininity just flew out the door right along with my …

"I'm so sorry." I said it again, this time sounding like I was pleading.

"What the hell are y'all up to—and don't tell me it's a damn cookout or whatever you said, Miss Vivi."

I cut my eyes to Vivi and shook my head. Miss Myra had built a reputation as a psychic in Tuscaloosa and she really believed in her talent. She would want to jump in to help solve the mission at hand. I took over.

"Oh, Vivi and I just wanted an out of the way place to chat where no one would bother us. With this baby fixin' to come we just wanted some time to reminisce. So we came out here. Really that's all." I smiled trying to be convincing, but I felt a tad nauseous. We desperately needed her to go. For a moment I wanted to ask her if she had seen any strange activity in the neighborhood but I knew I better save it. Having Miss Myra involved is not what we wanted. At least right now.

"Well, y'all sure do pick some off the wall spots. I

think I need to go, uhm, change my shoes here, they're soakin' wet. I'll see y'all later. The next time you need to use the potty, just come to my door, okay? No need to make an outhouse of your fine car, there, Miss Blake."

She trodded back to her car, shaking her head just as my cell rang. It was Dallas.

"What the hell are y'all doin' over there? Y'all gonna blow the cover if you keep playin' meet and greet with the neighborhood."

"I know it. Sorry." I knew she'd never believe me if I told her the whole squat and piss story.

"Oh my God," Dallas said into the receiver.

What?'

"It's her. There goes Jessica into the trailer. Let's go y'all. We'll be ready and waiting for your signal. Now, get in there and sell me some cupcakes!"

CHAPTER 19

Vivi and I looked at each other and took a simultaneous deep breath. The dust of the dirt road still swirled in the air as Miss Myra drove down to her trailer. Her light blue old model Chevelle stirring up red dirt as she drove.

"Okay, let's double check the plan," I suggested.

"We need to take our phones to use for pictures. Snap everything you can. Just silence it so no one will know," Vivi said

"I'll talk first and set it all up," I volunteered. "You say you need to meet everyone who lives there to see if they would like to volunteer for the bake sale at church. I'll make it up as I go and you watch me and I'll watch you. Let's just play along with each other. This may be our only shot."

"Ready?" Vivi asked. I wasn't but I knew it was now or never.

"As I'll ever be," I assured. "Let's get the cupcakes—and the bags for their donated clothes."

We gathered the items to help us pull off the trap and we headed up to the rickety stairs of the doublewide mobile home. I knocked as Vivi held the cupcakes.

"May I help you?" A little chubby woman with graying hair and big round blue eyes answered. She was in an old faded red dress with an apron. For a split second, I thought we could be at the North Pole and this was Mrs. Clause, surely not a bordello housemother.

"Yes, Hi-- we're from St. Catherine's. May we come in for a minute?" We both smiled at the lady.

" Uhm, certainly," she held open the door. "Y'all come on in and have a seat. I'm Myrtle Mays," she smiled. "Can I get y'all anything?"

Vivi and I stepped inside the tidy little place. The worn carpeted floor had a few old stains here and there but otherwise it seemed clean. To the left of the door was the kitchen. A step up led you to the galley styled cookery, counter-tops complete with nic-nacs and old cookbooks. It all looked normal. To the right of the front door stretched the family room. The shag, harvest gold wall-to-wall carpet led to the back of the room then up a narrow dark hallway. Vivi and I sat down on light blue, velveteen recliners. The plump little lady sat down on the dark blue couch opposite us.

"What can I do for y'all today?" she asked, folding her hands in her lap and offering a smile. I looked around and listened—no sounds of activity and no one else was even present. But Dallas had just seen the young dark haired Jessica come inside. I was really puzzled.

"Ma'am?" She leaned forward asking me again.

"Oh, Yes," I said Vivi nudging me. "Yes, I'm so sorry. We're here on behalf of St. Catherine's Catholic Church. These cupcakes are for you and yours if we can get you to join us in our annual clothing drive for women. We need blouses and really anything to help local women join the workforce. Also there will be a bake sale in a few weeks with all the proceeds going to charity and we still need volunteers. Would you mind taking a minute to see if you have anything you'd like to donate? And if I could, I would like to talk with any other women who might live here."

"Sure, y'all wait right here," she said. "I can't let y'all up the hall or anything. I have comp'ny here this week and they're still suffering jetlag, so everyone's asleep. I'll be right back." The round woman got up and made her way down the hall and slipped into the darkness. For a minute I wondered if she even knew what might be going on behind a few of those closed wooden doors.

"Vivi we need to get something. Look around. See anything?" I was starting to worry we were gonna blow it.

"No. I don't see a damn thing."

Dallas sent me a text. "*Anything?*"

"*No*," I sent back, "*not yet*"—trying to keep hope alive.

"Look," Vivi said. "Here's a Bible."

"A Bible? Wow. I wonder if we might have the wrong place?" But actually it was a good decoy for a whorehouse. Who'd think there was anything out of the ordinary going on in here? In fact, this little place was the most ordinary place I had ever seen.

Just then, Vivi picked up the Holy Book, her curiosity getting the better of her.

"Oh, Lord," she exclaimed. "This is no bible!" The book fell open and out fell a little black notebook. The entire inside of the bible had been carved out. It actually was a decoy--a fake book that hid the secrets, I hoped. Here we go.

"Put it in your purse," I whispered. "Quick!" Vivi shoved the black book into her red leather bag and put the bible back down on the little wooden lamp table next to her recliner. I heard the woman shut a door and head back down the hall toward us in the living room.

"Act normal!" I pushed. "Here she comes!"

"I'm sorry y'all, this is all I have." She handed over a couple of blouses and a pair of dress black pants. "I got way too fat for these and my kids still think of me as a size twelve. Hell, I need at least an eighteen these days." She laughed a hardy laugh as she dropped them into my bag. "They all still have the price tags so they're new. I never wore them."

Can this lady be for real? She was so sweet and wonderful, I wanted to take her home and make her my aunt. Vivi and I squirmed. We needed more. We knew something was going on with the fake bible, but we sure didn't have enough to help Harry.

"Do you mind if I use the restroom? I'm so pregnant, I have to go all the time."

"Uhm...sure, I guess so." The lady seemed uncomfortable. Fidgety. "It's the first door on the left. Just be real quiet. My guests are sleeping."

"Okay, of course, thank you so much." I glanced at Vivi then headed up the hallway. I walked ever so quietly, so as not to... ahem, wake the guests. I sent Dallas a text that I was on search mode and to be ready. Vivi smartly engaged the woman asking her about pictures of her family on the wall. It kept her from watching me and seeing just where I was going. I didn't even know where I was headed but I knew it was our last chance and that slutty little Jessica was in here somewhere.

I purposely walked right past the bathroom, and opened the third door on the left instead of the second. As silent as a mouse, I slowly turned the brass knob of the door, barley giving it a gentle nudge.

Holy Santa! I was most certainly not at the North Pole with Mrs. Clause. And just what to my wondering eyes should appear? Jessica the intern, and her big naked rear!

CHAPTER 20

All I could think of was *take a picture*! I pulled my phone from my pocket and pressed my finger snapping about ten photos, one after the other before Jessica stopped her lap dance and turned. Her heavy-set "client" had his eyes closed as she gyrated on his bare legs, khaki pants and tighty-whities down around his knees. So attractive. Then she turned suddenly to me. She gasped and jumped to the right, exposing her customer.

Oh. My. God. —I knew this guy! Jessica was doing Bullhorn McGraw! Harry's opponent during the election!

"What the hell?" Jessica screamed and tried to stand then fell over sideways, her legs sprawled from side to side, her ass in the air, her patent red stiletto got caught in his underwear. She hit the floor leaving her heel wrapped in his undies. I just kept snappin' pictures as he tried to cover up.

"Get the hell outta here, he yelled as he stumbled trying to reach me. I snapped a few more just as Vivi rushed in with the little round Madame.

"Ohmygosh! Bullhorn!" Vivi pushed inside the tiny

room. "Isn't one Politian enough for you, you little slut?"

"I think I may see the set-up Harry's talking about right before my eyes," I announced. "Miss Jessica seems to specialize in the politicos."

Just then, Dallas and her cameraman, Daniel popped up right behind Miss Mays.

Jessica and Bullhorn struggled to pull up their pants. Well her thong needed to be uhm-- repositioned.

"Jessica?" Dallas began.

"Get that goddamned camera outta here, now!" Bullhorn screamed.

Jessica managed to get to her feet, one shoe on and one shoe somewhere—possibly still in Bullhorn's pants.

"Tell me about your, uhm—position here." Dallas continued going after her story in the midst of all the confusion.

"Jessica?" Miss Mays questioned. "I don't have a Jessica. This is my Jasmine. She's my—niece. Yes, my niece. She lives here."

"Jasmine? Aren't you Harry's D.C. intern? You're the spittin' image of the girl in the photos," Vivi asserted.

"I'll say," I added.

"But when I just called her Jessica she looked up at me and answered," Dallas reasoned.

"Yeah, well, uhm, I don't know any Jessica," the young woman said. "My name is Jasmine." She looked away toward Bullhorn.

"And you, Bullhorn! You should be ashamed. Does your wife know where you are? Uh huh—I doubt it." Vivi was on a roll. And the TV cameras were too. Bullhorn managed to stand, belting his pants while he tucked in his shirt. He was silent, red-faced and bug-eyed.

There was no mistaking it—this was our slutty little intern. Jessica stood in her shiny stilettos buttoning her blouse and looking anywhere but at any of us.

"Jessica, Jasmine, whatever you wanna be called, the question is, are you having an affair with Senator Harry Heart?" Dallas was relentless. I liked this side of her. At least *now* I do.

"Uhm, I—I don't know what you're talking about."

"Do you work for senator Heart in any way?" Dallas kept probing.

"I don't know who your talking about." Jessica was good--tough to crack. Not that she didn't like to *show* her crack. But that was a different talent. Just then we heard a commotion in the tiny hallway outside the bedroom. Someone was pushing through. I looked over and saw Sonny. He had Jay Johnson with him. Jay was head of VICE.

"Okay, everybody outside," Sonny announced. "I think we all got a little business to take care of. Miss Myrtle, Mr. Johnson needs to speak with you personally. Everybody else, out! Now!"

Sonny was so great at taking over and no matter what the awful situation at hand, this was turning me on. "How the hell did you know where I was?" I asked him innocently. I surely had no intention of him ever finding out Vivi and I were here.

"No, the question is what the hell are you even doing here?" he said looking at me as we followed the little crowd outside.

"Answer mine first," I said trying to wriggle out of this.

"I'm here on a tip and when I saw the news truck and then your car, I raced in here.

Bullhorn suddenly pushed past Sonny and me and opened the side door. There were no steps out that door as he quickly found out. This trailer is set up high and every door needs steps or you have to well jump out. Being 5'7" and nearly 280 pounds, jumping wasn't gonna be a good idea for Bullhorn.

"Just where the hell do you think you're goin'?" Sonny snatched him by his belt and basically saved him from breaking his ass on the dirt yard. Bless her heart; Miss Myrtle didn't even have any grass to speak of there.

Sonny looked at me. "We'll continue this little talk later." He gave me a half grin and headed outside with Bullhorn in tow. A little gathering had formed in the front yard, Dallas at center- stage as she kept trying to make Jessica talk. Jay Johnson of VICE had already cuffed Miss Myrtle and Jessica. It was enough that they had proof of the money being exchanged for sex with the pictures I took on my phone.

Then out of the corner of my eye, I saw a man in a dark suit walking towards us. His hands were in his pockets as he sauntered up to the crowd. It was Harry. He moved through us all straight over to Jessica.

"Jessica, why?" Harry seemed hurt. He trusted this hometown girl.

"It was him! Jessica looked straight at Bullhorn. "He was the one! He paid me to do it."

"What?" Harry and Sonny said together. We all couldn't believe Bullhorn had stooped that low and been so desperate to replace Harry in congress.

"Yes. He paid me to bring you down. He thought he would take your place if you were thrown out of office so he sent me there to frame you up in an affair." Jessica explained as she spilled the whole conspiracy.

Dallas had the story of the century. "Get all that Daniel?" She asked her cameraman.

"You bet," he smiled. And he kept right on rolling.

"How much did Bullhorn pay you, Jessica?" Dallas kept pushing.

"I think we need to get these three to the station and get 'em booked," Jay broke in. "No more questions for now. They got plenty to answer once we get 'em downtown." He took Jessica and Miss Myrtle to his squad car. Sonny pushed Bullhorn from behind over to Jay's car too. He shook Jay's hand and made his way back to me. Vivi and I were talking to Harry.

Harry looked a bit shaken but relieved. The burden was gone. His name would be cleared. "I'm so glad you believe me now," he said. "I knew she was up to something since she kissed on me all the time but only when there was a camera. I guess you never know who to trust."

"Now look you two," Sonny said as he arrived to our little circle. "You two could have gotten hurt doing this. Remember, a dead man was found out here just the other day. This was crazy dangerous! Who's idea *was* this anyway?" Vivi and I looked at each other. *"I'm not gonna tell, are you?"* I heard her mind speak loud and clear behind those emerald green eyes of hers.

"Well, I got a tip and the tipster said you two might even be out here. I took no chances, grabbing Jay, since this is all his department, I sent him to go on ahead while I called Harry and told him I'd pick him up. We came rushing—in case you two were in over your heads.

"No, we're fine. I just needed to get some info for myself," I said. "We never expected to find Jessica in the act itself. Just plain luck."

"Well good thing you did, I guess. All those phone pictures will surely come in handy," Sonny reasoned.

Harry leaned over to hug me. "I gotta get back to D.C. I promised Dallas an on-set interview over at WTAL and after that it's the redeye to Washington." Just as he hugged me I felt it. Warm water gushing past my knees.

"Uh, y'all. I think we may have more on tap for tonight

than that TV interview," I said, stepping back from Harry and looking down.

"Ohmygosh! You're water just broke!" Harry shouted.

"Get in the car. I'll call Kitty and Meridee. I'll call your doctor. Go!" Vivi quickly organized the situation.

"Come on baby. Our boy is on the way!"

"He's early", I cried. "I'm scared."

"Just a few weeks-- he's already a kicker. He'll be fine. I'll turn the siren on and we'll be there in no time!" Sonny hurried me to his waiting patrol car.

"Harry come on," Vivi said. "I know you don't wanna miss this." Harry and Vivi ran to her car and followed Sonny and me in the squad car. This was strange in a way. Harry would be there to see me give birth—but not to our son-- to mine and Sonny's.

CHAPTER 21

"Come on, baby, let's get you in here!" Sonny ran around to the other side of the car to help me get out and into the hospital.

"Miss Blake! What in the world are you doin' here? Ain'tchew early? That baby's in a hurry." Miss Wylie, at the admitting desk, said as I rushed into the hospital. She was a short round woman about sixty-five years old with poufy graying hair piled on top of her head in an unruly bun. I had called my doctor on the way. She said she'd get me set up with the room and call the hospital before I got there.

"Yeah, I know it, Miss Wylie. This baby of mine's gonna be in a hurry his whole life. Did my doctor call?"

"Yep, let's get you registered, sweetie-pie. Have a seat." I sat down as I felt my contractions begin. I was nervous but I looked over and Sonny was worse. I had never seen him like this—he was pacing back and forth, biting his nails. My strong, in charge homicide detective was coming apart right in front of me! He looked over to me and smiled a weak little grin. I needed to give him something to do or he was gonna gnaw his fingers completely off.

"Sweetheart," I beckoned. "I'm gonna need my bag. I have it packed and sitting by the bedroom door. Could you be a honey and run home and get it for me? I need it." He looked at me as if I had asked him to go get popcorn right as the Titanic struck the iceberg. He might miss the action.

"Baby, I'm gonna be awhile," I assured him. "The contractions are really far apart." I did need my bag. I had packed it full of my primpers. You know, my make-up to look perfect in all my pictures, my special brand new fuzzy socks, and my perfumed body lotion for Sonny to massage me and soothe me. My baby blue nightgown set with satin robe was also in my bag. I had prepared to be the princess giving birth to the future king. I *needed* my bag!

"Okay," Sonny finally agreed. "But don't you have our son without me, I'll be right back. Cross your legs." He leaned down and kissed my head and dashed through the automatic doors just as Harry and Vivi rushed in.

"I'm going to grab Blake's bag," Sonny said. "Don't you let her have this baby without me."

"I won't but hurry up," Vivi said as she passed. She hurried over to me sitting with Miss Wylie. Miss Wylie and Kitty had been friends for years, though Miss Wylie was a good bit older. She lived in Glendale Gardens and had grown up just down the street from Kitty.

"I called your mama and Meridee. They're on the way," Vivi said as she clutched my shoulder. "You nervous?"

"As a cat in a room full of rocking chairs," I answered, smiling at her. That was one of her famous metaphors.

"Well, don't be. I did it and you sure can too." She smiled at me.

"Okay, who is the husband?" Miss Wylie asked. I was jolted away from my visions of me in my silk robe holding my precious bundle while Sonny massaged me with the perfumed body cream. Technically I was still married to Harry. I took a deep breath.

"Harry Heart," I answered. Harry looked over at me from the chairs across the lobby. He seemed out of place but where he belonged all at the same time.

"Okay and he's the... father?" She kept typing without looking up.

"Uhm, no..." I mumbled, interrupting her.

"I see." She peered over her silver glasses at me. "Well, I need the name of the father."

"Sonny Bartholomew." I sat up straighter in my chair. I was proud this baby was Sonny's. Mine and Sonny's. But the pride was only momentary.

"Hmm," Miss Wylie spoke up. "So the father's name will go on the birth certificate. Sonny is the father but listed as spouse will be Harry Heart?"

"Yes," I said sliding back down in my chair. "That is correct." My plans weren't working out exactly as I had hoped. The baby was about three and a half weeks early. My divorce was supposed to be final next week. If the baby weren't so eager to get here then Harry wouldn't be in the mix. I had so wanted my baby born to me after the divorce. There would be no confusion. Harry wouldn't even be in this picture. But no, the universe was not cooperating.

"Okay, your room will be ready soon. A nurse will be here in a jiffy to help you. Don't move." Miss Wylie smiled as she got up and took my file to the nurses' station.

"Oh my Lord, that was so embarrassing," I said to Vivi.

"What—you think she never saw a case like yours before?"

"No, it's just that it's me—you know, the good girl."

"Baby, that ship has sailed."

"Thank you. That boost of self esteem is exactly what I

needed," I said dripping with sarcasm.

"Oh, sweet baby Jesus, I'm so glad our little one hasn't arrived yet. I wanna be in there watching my baby have her baby," Kitty announced, her bangle bracelets jingling as she waved her arms wildly.

"My baby girl's gonna be a momma!" Kitty was comin' unglued with excitement.

"Oh, sugar, I am so proud of you," Meridee leaned down and kissed my forehead.

"What's *he* doin' here?" Kitty asked gesturing to Harry.

"I'm her husband," Harry stood and said boldly. I knew he just wanted to get a rise out of Kitty but I was beginning to think this day could actually get worse. The clash of people and personalities was fixin' to make one sour soup.

Little did I know, it was about to get even more interesting.

"Oh, baby girl, there you are. We just heard. Kitty called us to make sure we had the nursery ready, and honey, we so do. You are gonna be so happy when you see what we did. We're here to decorate the birthin' room now!" Druid City Hospital would never be the same. The Fru Fru's had arrived.

CHAPTER 22

The contractions were coming now on a regular basis. I settled into my bed as my entourage set up camp. All but Sonny. I was now in one of those hideous hospital gowns with no back, my bare ass on the cool sheets. I lay back with visions of my silk robe dancing in my head.

"Hey, Miss Blake, well it looks like our little guy will make his own time," Dr. Partlow said as she entered the room. "Everybody out so I can see just when our boy will be here." She shut the door as they all stepped to the hallway.

"Who the hell are those two?" The Doctor asked, "and why in the name of God are they hanging fancy lights in here?" She asked as the Fru Frus twirled out into the hallway with everyone else.

"Oh, I'm sorry. They are my nursery decorators."

"Well, they *do* know you aren't gonna live *here* after the baby's born, don't they?"

"Yeah they just wanted the room to be festive for all the pictures," I explained.

"Where's Daddy?" She asked.

"Sonny's on his way. He ran home to grab my bag."

"Well he might need to use his siren if he wants to be here to greet his baby. This kid's in a hurry."

"Noooo," I begged. "Sonny told me to wait."

"Well, our boy here has other plans."

"I need to call him," I said full of anxiety. "I need my bag," I said, not even thinking of Sonny missing the birth. "It has my body cream and fuzzy socks." Dr. Partlow just looked up at me from between my raised legs and smiled. I knew she was right. I could feel the contractions getting closer together. Nothing was going along with my grand plan. I wanted to be a princess.

"Okay, I think he'll be here in the next hour or so. He's waiting for no one."

"And he's okay? I mean he's early and all. Is he too early? Is he in danger?"

"He's healthy as a future Crimson Tide football star. I mean Sonny does keep calling him his quarterback. His vitals look good. He's just ready right now. So we'll go with his timing. We really have no choice. You're water has already broken or we could try to stop the labor," she explained as she grabbed my chart from the end of the bed and wrote something down. "It's all gonna be okay, Blake." She smiled. "You're fixin' to be a mother. It's the greatest feeling in the world. Now I'll be back to check on you in a bit. Rest while you can." She patted my foot as she walked over to the door.

The minute she left, the Fru Frus dashed back inside and pulled out some fabric swatches.

"Honey child! Lookey here. We gotta show you this pretty pattern we found. Want us to cover something with it while we wait?" Coco was beyond his usual excited self. He pranced around the room holding the fabric over a chair then up against the walls as curtains. "Gor—geous," he sang out. Don'tcha just love it?"

"Oh, I do. I'm just not too sure *management* here will." Just then Vivi and Kitty and Meridee stepped in. I was relieved. My girls to the rescue.

"Need some water? Ice chips?" Vivi asked.

"Nauseated?" Kitty quipped. "Maybe I can find you some salt to lick."

"Y'all, the doctor said I can't have anything now. The baby will be here in an hour."

"An hour?" Vivi said in shock. "Sonny better get his ass here. I'll call him."

"No no," Kitty said to Coco. "That pattern's all wrong. We're havin' us a boy. I don't like the paisley or the chevron prints."

"Are they for real?" Vivi asked me, her face contorted and her eyebrows up. She was dialing Sonny. "Voicemail," she said. "I can't believe this is your baby birthin' room—those two are nuts." She shook her head as she tried Sonny again.

"Miss Blake," Jean Pierre announced. "We believe the Feng Shui of this room is all off. We're gonna need to move a few things. And don't you worry—all's just as you ordered at home—butter and baby blue stripes and nobody is paintin' any naked people on the walls anywhere in the entire room."

At this point, I didn't care. I just wanted Sonny here. The boys began shoving the chair over near the door and pushing a small table over to the other side near the window. Another contraction. Vivi saw me wince. She ran into the bathroom and emerged with a wet cloth. She stood at my bedside and wiped my brow as Kitty and the Fru Frus kept rearranging the room. Vivi called the nurse's desk and asked for ice chips.

"Okay, little mama. Won't be long now. Lets have some deep breaths," Vivi said.

I breathed in and blew it out just like they taught me in Lamaze class. And again, little blows like I was blowing out birthday candles.

"Where the hell's Sonny? I need Sonny!" *Blow. Blow. Blow.* "Where is he? I need my fuzzy socks"— *Blow. Blow. Blow.* "--And my pretty blue nightie and body cream"— *Blow. Blow. Blow.* "It's not supposed to be like this. I'm supposed to be a princess."

The contraction passed and I fell back against my pillows. My face was on fire and my feet were freezing.

"I know, sweetheart," Vivi reassured me wiping my forehead with the cool cloth. "You *are* a princess. Sonny will be here before you know it."

The door flew open and in came the nurse with a bucket of ice cubes. But she never made it to me.

"Good Lord!" She said as she tripped over the chair now in its new home—in front of the door, spilling all the ice cubes everywhere as she stumbled.

"Why the hell is that chair in front of the door? She shouted.

"Evidentially the room had bad flow," Vivi explained.

"Well, it's certainly got flow now, with all this ice. I'll be right back." The nurse headed back to the hall, rubbing her knee and limping as she went.

The door opened again slowly as Wanda Jo poked her head in. Wanda Jo was Harry's and my secretary at our law office. She was middle-aged with salt and pepper hair and average sized. She had been by our side from the day we had opened our practice about eight years ago. Wanda Jo had been handling the office while I had been out this week. Things had slowed down there since Harry won the election and I became pregnant. Still, I couldn't believe she was bringing me a file when I was fixin' to give birth.

"Hey Miss Blake, look at you. All ready to bring us a new baby. I'm so happy for you." She walked over sweetly and gave me a kiss on the cheek. I felt something was wrong as I looked at her eyes. They were brimming with tears.

"I hate this more than I can say-- but I think this is what you've been waiting for." She handed me a manila file folder. I had no idea what this was but hoped that maybe one of my cases finally settled. I opened the file and saw the words at the top. *Blake O'Hara Heart vs. Harry Heart in the dissolution of marriage.* I could barely speak. There it was, the words cutting through me like a cold knife. This was it. The universe had cooperated and it would finally be over. Was this just what I wanted?

Vivi realized what I had in my hands. She quietly ushered out the Fru Fru's and Kitty. Wanda Jo looked sullen. Harry and I were like her kids. She had taken care of both of us for so long. She smiled weakly at me and backed out of the room into the hallway. Harry came in as she left. He knew.

"I'll be right outside if you need me," Vivi said, heading over toward the door. "I think you two need a minute."

I had no idea what to even say. I could feel my baby pushing his way here. This was his day. His birthday. Would I always remember that this too was the day I ended my marriage to what was once my best friend and partner? I didn't know what to do, let alone what to say.

"So this is it." Harry thankfully spoke first, a small smile on his clean-shaven face.

"Yeah. It looks that way."

He stood there, hands in his pockets. He was dressed in a navy suit with a perfectly starched bright white oxford, his initials embroidered on his cuffs, and his gold cuff links shimmering in the afternoon light streaming in through the window. Harry was the best-dressed man I had ever known. His dark brunette hair, strands of silver glistened around his temples. It was styled like a model, pushed back over his forehead highlighting those steal gray-blue eyes. I looked into them, as he stood unable to say much more.

"Thank you, Blake," he said finally.

"For what?"

"For all the good years. There was a time when what we had was the best there was." His eyes were now wet with memories.

"It was, Harry. It was."

"I'm sorry," he offered. "I want you to know it was all me. You did nothing wrong. You gave me everything and I couldn't see it. I was blinded by ambition. I don't blame you one bit for running to Sonny. He's a good man, Blake. Just know this. I wasn't lying when I told you I still loved you the other day. I do. I will, for as long as I live. I will always love you."

My heart was in my throat. I couldn't believe how loving and decent he was. This was the Harry I married. He had so long been gone from me. I knew I would love him forever too. But I had a new life in front of me. And a love with Sonny that was so deep and solid. I knew I also wanted to not be married to another man when I pushed this precious baby into the world. He belonged to Sonny. And there was no room now for Harry in this picture. As much as I loved Harry and knew I would miss his fabulous style and confidence, I knew it was time. Time to sign and let the past fade as I turned the page.

"I will always love you too, Harry. Now go take care of us back here at home by being the best damn senator we ever sent to Washington." I wiped my eyes and handed him the file. He walked over to the table and took out his silver pen from his inside coat pocket. He paused for one more second, one more glance at me. He smiled with his lips pursed together and signed his name on the bottom line. Nothing was contested and we weren't fighting over anything. All of it had been what they call an amicable divorce—whatever that really means.

He walked back to my bedside, putting the file down on the tray table in front of me. He stared at me sweetly and handed me his pen.

"You don't have to do it," he teased lightening the mood a bit. But he knew. I signed my name as Blake O'Hara Heart for the last time. Our divorce was final. I closed the file and handed Harry back his expensive pen. Harry's eyes brimmed over, a teardrop falling from his cheek and hitting my forearm. With quivering lips, he leaned down and pressed his lips to mine, soft and slow. His tear stained cheek now pressed to mine.

"Have a good and happy life, my sweetheart. I'll always be here for you." The emotion was stuck in his throat.

"I'll miss you," I said, tears now flowing down my face as well. "And Harry, you have a happy life too. I want that for you." He rested his face against mine one last time before he pulled away. And with a squeeze of my hand, he was gone.

CHAPTER 23

"Okay Blake, it's not gonna be long now," Doctor Partlow informed me.

"No! Sonny isn't back yet," I explained. "This baby cannot come into this world with his daddy not here. I refuse to let him out. Somebody call him now!" I was headin' toward a complete conniption. "Get Vivi in here," I ordered.

Vivi came rushing in. "Good God that baby's in a hurry."

"I know it. Call Sonny. He's gonna miss it. Oh, Vivi he can't miss it! He just can't. What am I gonna do?" I whined. "I need him. What in the hell could be taking him so long?"

"I'm callin' him right now," Vivi comforted. "I know he's bound to be back here any minute. Probably out there parking the car. Now calm down, it's not good for the baby."

"Arrrgggghhhh," I screamed. Another contraction. "He's comin'. The baby's not waitin' on his daddy."

"No answer, sweetie. I'm sure Sonny's almost here."

"I need my fuzzy socks, *NOW!*" I was becoming Pregnant-Zilla. I was missing my whole princess-giving-birth moment.

"Oh my Lord, where in hell have you been?" Vivi shouted as soon as Sonny ran through the door.

"I'm so sorry babe," he uttered out of breath. "I didn't see a bag by the door except for this one by the back door. I went as fast as I could." He looked flustered and a nervous wreck.

"Sonny, he's comin' right now! I tried so hard to wait for you but I couldn't wait a bit longer. Thank God you're here!" I was panting and puffing. I couldn't stand this much longer.

Sonny stepped over to my bedside, clutched my hand and smiled reassuringly.

"Okay, where's my cute socks and my satin blue robe?" I was determined to be the princess. "Bring my bag over here, okay? Before another contraction hits me."

"Okay baby," Sonny said. He bent over and opened the bag. "Aw shit," Sonny blurted.

"What?" I asked.

"You're not ev'n gonna believe this."

"What? What?"

"Will a wrench do? Maybe some needle nose pliers?"

"No joking right now, please! You will not be using some tool set to help me birth this baby. Now just bring me my socks. And grab that body cream too."

"I wish I could, baby but the closest thing I got in here to body cream and socks is WD40 and some gloves. Shit! I'm so sorry. I grabbed my tool bag by mistake."

"Aggggghhhhhhh!"

"Please don't scream at me, sweetie-pie. It was dark in there and I was in a hurry. I'm here and how 'bout I just rub your feet instead?"

With that last contraction, Dr. Partlow announced, "Just a few minutes and we're gonna have us a new Alabama quarterback!" Nurses rushed in and everyone took their places. "Here we go y'all. Sonny, take your place and help her breathe. Just like we learned in class."

Sonny stood right by my head and counted the breaths with me.

"I love you, baby." He whispered. "You're doin great."

"I wanted my socks. I wanted to be a princess."

"You *are* my princess," he whispered.

I could have smacked him if he wasn't so cute. I could feel his cheek on mine, his end of the day beard scratchy and warm.

Vivi stood by with her took over with camera on her phone and recorded the entire thing from a discreet location.

Dr. Partlow positioned herself to catch my baby, like a quarterback waiting for the snap.

"Come on Blake, he's almost here. Push! I can see the head. I need another big push."

Aarrrgh! I yelled as I pushed my baby boy into the world.

"He's here, baby! Our boy! Our son! Ohmygod! I can't even believe this!" Sonny's face was wet with tears and rosy red. He had pushed with me the entire time.

I collapsed back onto the soft pillows of the bed. "He's beautiful," I managed, the salty perspiration catching on my lips. Joy filled me like I had never felt before.

Vivi got the whole thing on her camera phone-- my baby's first breath, and me and Sonny in our first collaboration.

"Oh, baby! I'm so proud of you," Sonny kissed my lips, his passion overflowed as he pressed his sweet face to mine. Before I knew it the nurse handed me my baby boy. His blue eyes staring into mine, a little stranger in my arms. But with one look into each other's eyes, I was totally in love. The protector in me came into full bloom, and there was a feeling that there was nothing on earth that I wouldn't do for this baby. Mama Bear. Now I know why we get called that. I would sacrifice everything for this little pink brown haired blue-eyed bundle. Suddenly I felt it. I had never ever known love like this. This overwhelming magnitude of love enveloped me and could not look up from his innocent blue eyes.

"What's his name?" Dr. Partlow asked.

I looked up at Sonny and smiled. He nodded. We had decided months ago if we had a boy, his name would be Beau, after Sonny's grandfather.

"Beau Bartholomew," Sonny said proudly. "Beau Brandon Bartholomew. BBB."

"That sure sounds like a ball player to me," the nurse said as she wrote the name down on my chart and she turned to walk out of the room.

"Oh, Blake he is just gorgeous," Vivi said leaning down to kiss my forehead. "He looks just like both of y'all."

With that in came Kitty and Meridee and the Fru Frus. Beau was a healthy eight-pounder and everybody wanted to see him.

The nurse had cleaned Beau immediately and checked him over thoroughly before handing finally back to me. A small crowd had gathered in the room, everyone peering at our precious new addition.

"Is that the most precious baby you have ever seen?" Kitty gushed.

"Oh, my gosh!" Meridee, exclaimed, "that beautiful baby boy looks just like one of mine. He's just a chubby little fella. And that button nose—Blake, he's your baby alright." Meridee took the baby in her arms and nuzzled him to her. I loved that sight--my precious Nanny holding my new favorite person. I was part of the chain now. A link in a long chain of mother's and babies. Part of yesterday and tomorrow all at once. This was the very most wonderful thing in the whole world. To be a mother, I thought. Whether you give birth like me, or adopt a precious little angel like Dallas, motherhood was a secret society...and now I was in the club. Nothing had ever felt so right in my life.

Suddenly I realized Kitty was a saint. All mothers are saints. And I would go through the swing of hormones, the pressures of being a woman trying to have it all, the frustrations of it all--just so I could experience motherhood. It would all be worth anything to carry life inside me and to give life to my child. *My Child*. I loved the sound of saying it.

Lewis walked in grinning ear to ear. His big dimples deeper than ever, with his little Tallulah in his arms. She was about three months old and looking more and more like her mama every day. Vivi took her little pink sweetheart and introduced her to Beau.

"Sugar, meet your new boyfriend," Vivi said smiling at me, a tear glistening in her eye. "You are always gonna love this boy. Your mama already does."

"I'm not so sure he would date an older woman," I teased Vivi.

"Oh, Blake, we're mother's. Can you believe this? I love this day. I have thought of it since we were barely teenagers. I love you so much." She leaned over and kissed my forehead.

Dallas peeked her head inside the door from the hallway, and clutching her hand to the tiny hand of her little blonde girl, she made her way to my bedside. "I'd like y'all to meet my new daughter, Sara Grace."

"Oh, Dallas, Congratulations," I said. That's

wonderful."

"Your baby is so cute," Sara Grace said, gently stroking Beau's forehead.

"Welcome to the family sweetie-pie." I said smiling at the sweet little child.

"It's not a hundred percent settled yet with all the papers," Dallas explained, "but she can live with me until it's official. She's finally mine." Dallas was glowing nearly as much as I was.

"I have to tell you girls, I am pretty proud of us today," Vivi said joining us. "We pulled off quite the sting. I know people think I'm a tad crazy but, seriously y'all--I think we are quite the investigation team."

"I'm pretty proud of us myself," Dallas responded with a grin.

We certainly did make quite a team. Even I was proud of us all pulling this off together to help Harry get back to the Capitol and clear his name. We all smiled at each other in that moment. Sassy Sleuths. Maybe there was a future in that.

"We can open the blinds now," Dr. Partlow said. "Everybody's decent."

Vivi walked over to the window to the hallway and twisted the rod, only to see Harry still in the walkway. She looked over at me. My eyes caught Harry's when everyone else was looking and cooing at Beau as he lay now in my arms. I held my baby and I smiled sweetly at Harry as he kissed his first two fingers and pressed them to the glass. He smiled softly at me and winked as he walked away. I watched him head to the elevator until he was out of sight.

THE END

Acknowledgements

Thank you seems so small and insufficient when I think of all who have held me up with love, motivation and encouragement. My friends and family-- where would I be without all of you? My writer friends, you are especially wonderful! Robyn Carr, your priceless hilarious conversations have kept me believing, and laughing so hard, you have been such a wonderful friend, and a life-saver for me. You are one of the strongest women I have met. Thank you for sharing so much of yourself with me. I treasure you and our friendship! Jane Porter, you have been so sweet and encouraging. I can't thank you enough for including me in your book signings and wrapping your arms around me with love and belief in me—you welcomed me into your circle like an old friend. I can't thank you enough—I am thrilled to be part of Tule Publishing and to be asked to write your Carolina Born series!! Thank you sweet Jane! Bella Andre—Oh my goodness! Where do I begin? This novella would not even exist without your motivation and encouragement. Your guidance and the time you have spent with me are truly priceless!! "Go Forth and Conquer, you cheered, and I am out of the gate and on my way. How can I ever thank you? Kim Boykin, you have been such a source of joy and cheer for me and I love our "blossoming" friendship as we set forth to create Carolina Born together with all the Bloom sisters! Andrea Hurst, you have held my hand through some of my hardest months—you are a forever friend!! You are all the most special women—I am so proud to be able to call you my friends. To my sweet family, especially my mother, Betty, my cheerleader in all things, my best friend and sidekick, I love you more than words can do justice. My precious son, Brooks, I love you so much, my relationship with you is what I am most proud of in my life—I'm so proud of you and our close relationship and friendship, I could burst. You will always be the best part of me. To my husband, Ted, you are the most patient man in the universe—thank you with all my heart for always putting up with all my—uhm—stuff. You are my love and my sweetheart—what would I ever do without you? I am so happy you kept knocking on my door all those years ago in college! I love you always and forever. To my Aunt Patsy, thank you for all the love and the constant support. You have been such a huge support—I love you so much. A huge part of me is all you, as I idolized you as a child. Corey, my nephew, Thank you for being my assistant and my driver all summer on my book tour and for making sure Nanny was always taken care of while I met my readers—I love you so much! You are priceless and so special. To the rest of my family you know how much I love you—you are my whole heart. To my friends—Susan, you are beyond wonderful—thank you for letting me stay with you when I am home—nothing could be more special than time with you, your family, Greg and Matt especially. I love y'all so much! Lynn, what in the world would I doo without my sane voice? You are and always have been such a priceless special person—one of a kind—with you, I always have my very own "Vivi"—I love you dearly! And my precious Steve Phillips, who took my book up 20,305 feet up the Himalayas –I am forever in love with you—you will be by my side till eternity and you have made sure I will always know this. I can't even put into words what your friendship means to me. I know all I have to do is call and you will be there. Some friends, the souls just "know" and you are that friend for me. Thank you with all my heart for all you are to me. To my fabulous technical support system, Jeremy West, my cover designer, web designer, and all around uber talent—you are amazing! Thank you for all the late night texts, emails and basically being there whenever I have more "amazing idea" I'd like you to try! You are more than my designer you are also my trusted friend! Thank you Kristen Freethy, my book assistant, for everything—especially your friendly, cheerful, patience at walking me through the e-publishing world and making it seem so easy. I am so happy you have my back as I walk into the unknown wood—holding your hand has made it much less scary! I have so many others I love and want to thank I could write an entire book just filled with people I love and appreciate. I am so lucky for that! As always, thank you with all my heart for the unconditional love and support of my hometown of Tuscaloosa Alabama. As always, I hope I make y'all proud.

Meet Beth Albright

Beth Albright is a Tuscaloosa native, former Days of Our Lives actress, and former radio and TV talk show host. She is a graduate of the University of Alabama School of Journalism. She is also a screenwriter, voice-over artist and mother. She is the mother of the most wonderful brilliant son in the universe, Brooks and is married to her college sweetheart, Ted. A perpetually homesick Southern Belle and a major Alabama Crimson Tide fan, she splits her time between San Francisco and, of course, Tuscaloosa.

Beth loves to connect with her readers.

Visit her online:
http://www.thesassybelles.com

Facebook:
https://www.facebook.com/pages/The-Sassy-Belles/202653853110065

Twitter:
https://twitter.com/BeththeBelle

Goodreads:
https://www.goodreads.com/author/show/6583748.Beth_Albright

50822029R00077